Mazie's a se  le. She knows that, of course, and does an excellent job of hiding it.

Then, there's Sk'doo. Something less than a ghost, it's doing its thing, zooming around its cemetery, listening to Deads. Its routine changes when a body is placed in a nearby pond. In learning how it happened, Sk'doo discovers its Quick friend, Kaz, is in danger.

Who's Kaz? She's lonely, afraid, and confused. She's ghosting her way through life, preferring the peace of a cemetery to the pain of living. At least until Sk'doo causes her to meet Mazie who brings light and excitement.

Mazie is manipulative, opinionated, and cunning. She decides to "educate" Kaz, taking delight in creating a series of uncomfortable situations for her more-than-willing victim. Kaz begins to blossom and falls hard for her new friend.

All the same, Sk'doo must warn Kaz of the danger Mazie brings. The problem is how, when Kaz has no idea Sk'doo exists.

THE QUICKS, THE

DEADS, AND ME

Don Hilton

A NineStar Press Publication
www.ninestarpress.com

The Quicks, The Deads, and Me

First Edition, July 2024

ISBN: 978-1-64890-778-4

Also available in eBook, ISBN: 978-1-64890-777-7

CONTENT WARNING:
This book contains sexual content, which may only be suit-
able for mature readers. Depictions of the death of a sec-
ondary character, death of a child, references to suicide,
references to self-harm, homophobic slurs, transphobic
slurs, grooming, and forced outing.

For Gail, her Keith, my Gus.

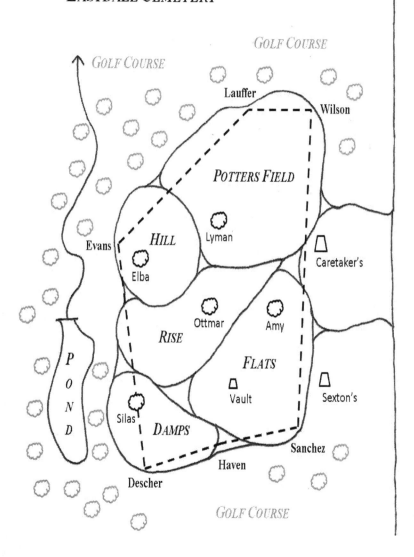

EASTDALE CEMETERY

To Start...

I AM STRONG and my burden isn't heavy but carrying it up the creek is proving a bit more difficult than I anticipated. Poor planning on my part. Still, having it wrapped in black landscape cloth and bound with old nylon rope helps. Considerably.

The biggest problem would be the dark, if not for the full moon. Then again, transporting a corpse across a golf course in the middle of the day is probably not A Good Idea.

Though, I've never liked the word "corpse." It lacks elegance. Remains? Maybe. Cadaver? Definitely not! Deceased? Departed is better. I smile to myself.

I've surveyed this stream more times than I care to

remember, accidentally-on-purpose hitting so many shots into it from so many fairways that the others in my regular foursome have taken to calling it my "ball magnet." Its high banks make it perfect for a nighttime transit of the landscape. The gravelly bottom provides easy walking and doesn't show footprints. It's always dry this time of year unless there's a big storm. Going under the half-dozen small bridges that crisscross it for the course and dodging the spiders is a pain, but a small price to pay for the otherwise easy access to the pond at the far end.

I stop for a moment as I enter the woods. I've made better progress than I planned. It's a shame I can't reuse this location, but that would be lazy and sloppy. I must avoid both.

There's breeze enough to keep the mosquitos at bay but not discourage the lightning bugs. It's beautiful—clear and starry. I'd probably see the Milky Way were it not for the moon and the lights of the big-box parking lot outside the nearby hick town. A wonderful night for a burial at sea...at pond, anyway.

The frogs quiet as I arrive, then resume their chorus. I place my burden on the ground. Gently. Gently. Always gently.

It smells wet here. Water seeps from between the thick, wide, moss-covered boards making up the spillway of the small dam forming the pond. I tie the ropes to the old cement blocks I'd carried and hidden as a test run a few nights before.

As I prepare to place the departed in the water, I notice the cloth has slipped a bit from around the left side of the face. A sweet ear and the jewelry piercing it shows through the gap: a simple gold ring with a small white diamond and dark ruby, one above the other. I softly tuck both under their cover and tug and fold the material back in place, making sure it looks just right.

This one is prettier than usual and doomed from the first hello. Certainly beyond my initial question. "May I sit here?"

It's always the first thing I say and starts the dance that is the beginning of their end. It's always quick, with death as a surprise, as it should be. Unconscious in seconds. Gone in minutes.

Even though the night's warm, I shiver at the memories.

One last running of my hands over the body, nude and oh-so-clean within the dark cloth. Then, taking care to not disturb the frogs, I ease the bundle with its weights into the deep blue-green water.

Ashes to ashes, dust to dust, and all that mumbo-jumbo. Except when there's so much moisture involved, it's mostly mud.

The departed disappears without so much as a splash. A mass of bubbles rises to the surface, then tapers off.

Another beautiful creature gone, but not forgotten. Transformed into food for the turtles, which is fine because I like turtles too.

I sigh. I'll be calm now, for a while. I'll visit until I get bored. Then, I'll start my preliminary scouting which will, as it always does, turn up another object worth collecting.

When that happens, the dance begins again.

But, for the moment, I can forget about all that.

I turn and head downstream with a grin. My golf scores are destined to improve now that I can avoid the water hazards.

Chapter One

SK'DOO

"Things are different when you see the other side."
    "Cousin Freddy is the smartest of us all."
    "There's no use arguing, I just won't do it."

I call myself Sk'doo. Not because it's my name, but because I know everything is called something and I'm part of everything, so I need to be called something. It's early morning in this place where I am. As usual, just the Deads and me. But that'll change when the Quicks begin to arrive.

Quicks always do the same things the same way, so the first is due soon, running. After that, it'll be the one with the dog, walking. Then the caretaker, if they're working. After that, any number of Quicks throughout the light of day.

And, sure enough, here's the first Quick: Lady Runner. For years she has passed through almost every early morning. When her hair's long she pulls it back from her face, especially when the weather's warm.

I have no legs, so I've never run. But I wonder about it. Wondering is one of the things I do. I know Lady Runner enjoys gliding through her every-morning circuit of Outside Road. Her face is calm. I hear her breathing, but it's not labored. When the kind-of-portly Quicks run, it looks painful, but they do it anyway.

I have something I suppose is pain, that hurts, but when it hurts, I stop. I used to feel it only during lightning storms which always make me zoom to hide. But that changed when they started stringing cables on the tall posts on the far side of Roadway. Even though I can't get too close, I feel zings from them too.

"In-out-in-out-in-out. The cats are worse than kids!"

Besides the lightning and the cables, the zing comes from machinery. Now, it comes from the Quicks.

I enjoy being near Quicks. Feeling what they feel and helping them find calm. Now, it hurts to approach most of them. It started with the watches they wear and grew from there. Lady Runner, for instance, carries a box and has small objects in her ears that cause zings. So, I keep away.

I don't know what the zing-things are, exactly. I know Quicks talk to them and voices come from them. Music too, sometimes. But I can't get close enough to know because they hurt and I don't do things that hurt.

I am fascinated by Quicks, even when I have to keep my distance. But though I like, wonder about, and help them, I don't know them.

What I know are the Deads.

*

"I like it when you kiss me like that."

"Don't get near Buddy. That dog farts!"

"Yes, shrimp are treyf. *I still eat them."*

I don't remember not being here. I sometimes wonder if I am here. I don't know what I'm supposed to do. But I know what I do during the time I'm somewhat certain I'm here.

I listen to the Dead—just listen.

I used to try to talk to Deads but gave up when I came to know they don't listen. I wonder if, maybe, because Quicks don't listen.

Deads talk all the time. They don't all talk all the time, or all talk all at once. It's just that there are plenty of Deads, so one of them is bound to be talking. I used to think they waited until I was near to speak but now I wonder if they talk when I'm not around. Not that it matters, because I'm the only one listening.

"Get out of that tree before you fall and break your neck."

I remember everything I hear, from both the Quicks and the Deads. I know what I know of Quicks because of what they feel, say, and do. With Deads, it's all what they have to say.

Deads don't say all they have to say all at once. It comes out a little at a time. They don't tell stories. They don't tell things in order. And they repeat—all the time—they repeat. But if you listen and remember, you can put things together.

A few things about Ezme Evans, for example: Ezme holds Edge on Hill. She became Quick in 1824 and Dead in 1828. She spoke and knew her letters by the time she was walking and reading and doing numbers before catching Summer Disease. Her favorite colors are blue and yellow, the name of her favorite cat is "Skipper," and her papa calls her "Peapod." Her last words as a Quick were, "I see where I am going." Ezme has never said what she saw or where she was going as she moved from Quick to Dead. Maybe, some-day, she will.

It takes a while to learn about any Dead. Some of them talk right away. Some of them hardly ever do. What they say usually comes slow and gradual, like water seeping into stone.

I wonder if, maybe, I'm a stone.

*

KAZ

I decide, again, that I don't like my face. My nose is too big, my eyes too small, my chin too round, my ears too floppy. I'm also too tall and too skinny. Shouldn't forget those, I suppose.

I sigh. It could be worse. I hardly left the house when I had pimples *and* braces at the same time. At least now my skin's clear and my teeth are straight. But I still hardly leave the house.

Even though my teeth are straight, I don't smile much because, when I do, my gums show, but I'm working on that. I practice in the mirror: I smile without showing my teeth. I smile showing some of my teeth. I shut my eyes, smile, then look. Gums!

My hair is boring brown. My choices are to grow it long enough to weigh down the massive cowlick behind my floppy left ear or cut it short enough to hide the cowlick. Wear it long and my eyes are smaller and my chin rounder.

Wear it short and my nose is bigger and my ears even flop-pier. At least it's not super-tight like Mom's is and Dad's used to be.

GeeGeema says my hair's curly from all the ornery I have in me and that I'll grow into my face. I know the first part isn't true because I have no ornery, and I'm sure the last part won't be good.

GeeGeema, she's Mom's-mom's-mom. She's old-old but is in pretty good shape, besides being almost blind. She was able to read when she first got here, but now she only sees some light and dark and a little bit up close. Macular degeneration does that.

She doesn't talk about what else is wrong, other than saying she's just plain wore out. She sings made-up songs to her fat black-and-white cat, Preston. She also dozes in her chair and listens to hockey or golf on the TV.

It cracks me up that she loves hockey and golf so much. She never skated or hit a golf ball in her life.

She gets around okay and likes to go for car rides, espe-cially for ice cream, but she's really slow. We have to be pa-tient because she speaks her mind if rushed. She speaks her mind all the time.

I smile, then adjust to hide my gums.

I wasn't happy when GeeGeema and Preston moved in a couple of years ago. They took my bedroom, and I moved into what we used to call "the big closet." Now, I like my little room with its tiny window, and love GeeGeema more than anybody. She's funny and serious, mean and kind, and smart and goofy. All at once. She understands me when nobody does, and she's one of only a couple people I can really talk to.

But Preston, her old fat cat? We leave each other alone. I have a set of three scars on the back of my right hand to remind me why I don't pet him. He's old, but he's faster than me. My chores include feeding him and cleaning his litter box. GeeGeema calls it "servicing both ends" and always laughs when she does.

"Good morning, glory," she says in her whispery voice when I round the corner into the living room. She's always up and dressed before me, sitting in her chair in front of the window, with a small table between her and the next chair. "How'd you sleep?"

"Okay, GeeGeema. It was hot last night, huh?"

She chuckles. "I slept with two blankets. I don't feel the heat like I used to. So, you gonna stand there with your teeth hanging out or you gonna give an old lady a hug?"

"No hugs with Preston in your lap."

She shoos the cat away. "Go on, you old thing!"

With Mr. Claws out of the way, I lean over and hug her. Not too hard because it always feels like she might break.

She peers up at me, tilting her head and looking off to the side like she does when she wants to see what little she can. "You look good this morning and your hair is so nice."

She reaches up and touches the mess behind my ear, smiles, and tells me for what seems like the millionth time, "You recall that your granddaddy had a cowlick just like that, when he had hair."

"Yes, GeeGeema, I recall." He died before I was born.

Preston purrs as he winds his way around my legs. That's a sure sign he's expecting food. I go to the kitchen and pick up his licked-clean bowl from the floor next to the stove. From the cabinet under the sink, I grab a green can of stinky-chicken cat food. He sits and starts to meow as soon as he hears it crack open.

"Only a half-can, now, we don't want him getting fat!"

"Yes, GeeGeema," then to Preston, I mutter, "too late for you."

"What was that, baby?"

"I was talking to the cat," I say more loudly. "I said 'here's your plate for you.'"

He digs in as soon as I plunk the bowl on the floor. How he eats the stuff, I'll never know, but he loves it as long as it's stinky-chicken in the green can. Not the stinky-chicken in the red can. Or the stinky-chicken in the blue can. Nope. He hates those.

I take the half-empty green can, seal it in a plastic bag, and put it in the fridge for Preston's 3:30 meal.

I walk around the corner and kneel beside GeeGeema's chair. "Mom and Dad are at work..."

"I know. I'm old, not stupid!" She grins.

"I have to go to the store for a few hours. You'll be okay while I'm gone?"

She smiles. No teeth. I can't figure out how she eats apples. She only wears her dentures when we go out. "Don't you worry. Preston and me will keep each other company. But could you please fetch me a little water before you go?"

"Sure." I walk back to the kitchen and pull a heavy coffee mug from the cabinet. GeeGeema needs to feel where things are, so everything has to have a wide base or she'll tip it over. I should know; she knocked a glass of water onto my phone last month. She felt really bad and offered me some money to help buy a new one, but I refused to take it. I should've known better since I'd seen her tip tall glasses over before.

Besides, I have a job. I can help pay for a replacement.

I pause before taking the water to her, looking at her face from the side. I've seen pictures of her when she was young. Tall, straight, and pretty. It's hard to believe she was once like that. The only thing that's the same is her hair, still in short ringlets, like mine, except instead of dark, it's pure white.

I walk over to her.

"Right here, in the middle"—she pats her table—"so I know where it is."

I give her another hug. She cranes her neck a bit to rub her cheek against mine, then sits back with a sigh.

"You be careful, going to work. Do good once you get there."

She always says the same thing.

"Yes, GeeGeema. Bye-bye."

"And I love you too!"

That's something else she always says.

*

SK'DOO

"I am that child's father."

"He loves me, but I don't care."

"My butt's too big."

I watch the gravediggers prepare the earth for a burial.

Before the machines I enjoyed visiting with the gravediggers, listening, learning: the right way to hold a shovel, how to predict the weather, baseball, football, beer, what made a lady pretty, why the boss is almost always dumb.

"My jellies always won blue ribbons."

I knew all the names of all the Quicks who worked here. Through time, several families lived in Sexton's. I knew them and their animals, especially a black dog, Jigs. I watched many of those Quicks grow old, and now I listen to them.

The Sextons' children and their friends played among the Dead. They're the reason I know foot races, hide-and-seek, tag, cowboys-and-Indians, how to ride a bike (at least the idea of it), what candy is, how much fun it is to chew gum and blow bubbles, how skinned knees hurt, what rubber and glue do, why someone looking at you is something worth complaining about, tattletales, and why moms and dads are almost always dumb.

Children are the best teachers. They've taught me colors, along with letters and numbers. With the last two, I figured out how to read. There were silly things: "Ink-a-dink a bottle of ink. The cork fell out and you stink!" Songs about gopher guts. And important things: Which boys are cutest. Why girls have cooties.

I wouldn't know a cootie if I saw one, but it's girls who seem to have them. I also know how to give shots against them. And boys are ugly and stupid. I know that too. As far as who's best, girls or boys—it was never decided.

"Pull the cart to the curb—the step's too high for Mother." This new grave is being dug in Flats. It's nowhere

near Edge, which is all right, but I wish it was far enough out to stretch it because Edge determines how far I can wander, and it hasn't moved in a long time.

Edge runs between the outermost graves. I can't get around it and there's no arguing with it. A little bump is fine, just a tingle. A push feels like lightning. Bad lightning, up close, on top of me, overwhelming. I know better than to zoom, full speed, into Edge.

When the Dead were few, and there was very little room to wander, I hated Edge. Now, with so many Deads, and all of them talking, there is so much to do that Edge doesn't seem so bad.

Some days I don't like being kept here, but I'm not sure what I'd do if I could wander where I wanted.

I'd like to see more of where the Quicks live and what they do when they're not here, but if I did, who would listen to the Dead? And if the cables on the poles are any clue, the world away from here is filled with lightning.

"The gas bill is late. Why is the gas bill always late?"

I can't get close to the diggers because of the machinery and their lightning-boxes so I'll keep a safe distance, near Hannah Griggs who's on the Rise side of Damps. The ground here is filled with cracks from it being so dry but grows soft after a hard rain. Deads don't care about such things.

A few things about Hannah: He was Quick starting in

1892 and Dead in 1910. He's from a place named Kalispell, Montana, and his family moved here when he was too small to remember. He broke his neck falling from a wagon just after midnight on what was the start of his eighteenth year. He knows he's not living up to his family's expectations of what they want from a daughter. He has kissed a number of young men, but never fancied any of them. He also says he hates wearing women's undergarments.

"Touch my ass again and I'll kick you straight in the nuts!"

Deads tell me all kinds of things.

*

KAZ

I love Eastdale Cemetery. It's another reason everyone thinks I'm weird. Most days, going to or from work, I ride through it, being careful of the squirrels that are always around.

I first started hanging out here when I was really depressed. GeeGeema hated me spending so much time with the dead and wasn't shy about telling me so. Maybe she was right, then, because I would hide by myself on the bench over by the big sycamore and cry. But after a while, I didn't think of this place in that way. I feel calm and safe here.

Sometimes, after work when it's cooler, I stop and look at the stones. I've seen them enough times that they're starting to be like friends. There are so many different kinds. Old ones, new ones. Some of the old ones have strange first names: Thacker, Salmon, Ezme—she was only four when she died. There are so many kids, but lots of old folks too. I saw online that people in Potters Field were too poor to have stones. I hope somebody remembers them.

I like that I almost always see the same people here, like the old guy with the beard who I passed at the caretaker's entrance. He always says the same thing, "beautiful day," no matter the weather. It's funny. This is supposed to be a sad place, but all the people I see are smiling.

The cemetery's outside road is paved and there are hardly ever any cars. I like to see how far I can go, no hands. I can even make it up the hill that way, if I'm going fast enough at the bottom, but this morning a car goes by and I have to grab the handlebars.

I coast down the other side of the hill, no hands, but slow where they're digging a grave. I wonder who it's for? I'd like to stop and see what they do, but I never would. Besides, I have to get to the store.

*

SK'DOO

"I think my big toe will plumb fall off."
  "People like that can't be trusted."
  "I don't want to die and go to hell."
Here comes Young No Hands on their wheel. That Quick started visiting not too long ago and used to sit on the bench near Silas and cry. Sad Quicks like that bench. It's shady and cooler there, back and away from the road, and I suppose hard to see. Kissing Quicks like it too, probably for the same reasons.

I know about crying Quicks, so I sat and helped as best I could. What Young No Hands felt was easy for me to feel and so I was able to help more than usual. I can't always understand why Quicks cry but in this case, it was loneliness. I know about that too, because it's just me here most of the time. Along with a whole bunch of talking Deads.

"It'll be over when I pull the trigger."
Now, Young No Hands doesn't cry, but they sometimes walk among the Dead. Very often they have no lightning-box, or it's not working, and I stay alongside. They don't search for any one Dead but repeat the names and numbers of many as they go, and I can practice my reading. We both get something from the other and that's good. They don't cry so much, but I still feel their loneliness.

"Two-cycle engines aren't worth a damn."

There's White Beard Old Man walking down the hill. His first name was Red Beard Young Man but that changed with passing time. He always takes Outside Road before the sun is at its top, but he walks far more slowly than he used to.

He never has a lightning-box, so I move to him. He always looks calm, but his feelings usually don't match. He often talks to nobody. I wonder if he sees something I cannot.

I can't follow him closely on the road in Damps because Edge won't let me, but I can visit when he's where I can reach. He'll probably stop to talk to the gravediggers, because he always talks to everyone he sees. I'll stay back, away from the machine, until he moves away from there.

*

MAZIE

I'm making my first visit today. It's warm, but cloudy, with a nice breeze to keep the bugs away.

Approaching via the dry stream is out of the question so this is the only way I can be close. I also gain extra enjoyment from the public passing so close to my secret yet never knowing what they're missing.

I don't like cemeteries. I have no objection to death on

an individual basis, especially when I'm involved. I enjoy spending time with those I've helped cross over, but death presented on a larger scale isn't my cup of tea. It's a reminder that no matter how careful I am with myself, somewhere like this is where I'm bound to end up!

The place is surprisingly small. I could walk from one side to the other in less than ten minutes. But I don't walk, I drive the paved, outside road, along the woods, in a counterclockwise direction. There's an empty section, first. As I go, I can see the golf course through breaks in the trees.

I swerve around an idiot kid riding no hands as the road swings up, around a small knoll covered with old, dirty, and tilting monuments. It's all so shamefully decrepit. I take good care of my dead. Does nobody else care about their own?

As the paved road drops from its highest point, a gravel track comes in from the left where I can park. When I do, the kid on the bike passes by.

Here's the bench on the right, looking down over a steep embankment to the spillway end of the pond. I was a little worried it might be moved since I last checked out the place, but it's just as I remember. Excellent.

I exit the car, sit, look a bit, then close my eyes, breathe deeply, and remember: looks, touches, aromas, sounds, movements. The sudden struggle. Rapid heartbeat fading to peace. Then bathing, primping, perfuming, posing, photo-graphing. Wrapping, tying, transporting, carrying. That last run of my hands over the body before sliding it into the pond. My fingertips tingle and I rub them against my thumbs. I take in a breath, hold it, and slowly exhale.

"Beautiful day!"

I swivel my head to see some old guy with a beard coming toward me. "Excuse me?"

"I said 'beautiful day!'"

"Y-yes," I stammer, "beautiful day." Then, under my breath, "Beautifully ruined by an idiot."

On my way out, I see the old fool wasting the time of two workers who are supposed to be digging a grave. The kid on the bike is long gone.

*

KAZ

I don't mind work. It's okay. Sometimes the boss seems dumb, but I suppose all bosses are dumb, sometimes.

There's nothing *that* hard about working in the store, other than being careful not to drop stuff. Customers won't buy damaged cans or boxes, even when the food is perfectly good. The boss sometimes lets us take damaged containers home. He's not so dumb, then. Trouble is, I never like what's dropped.

I remember Jimmy dropping a box of sweet pickles. Twelve small jars. That was a mess. We mopped the floor but could never get it completely unsticky. It's still a little sticky. It'll probably be sticky forever.

Jimmy and I are opposites: He's short and I'm tall. He's kind of chunky and I'm skinny. He talks all the time and I don't. He's funny and I usually mess up jokes. He's good-looking and I'm not. He's careless and I'm very careful. He thinks he's faster than me and I know he's not.

Jimmy has lots of friends and he treats me like all the rest of them. To him, I'm not weird. I'm just me. We're not best friends or anything. I don't have any best friends.

I park my bike against the back of the building, beside Jimmy's old beat-up wreck. Just inside the side door is the job sheet, listing what needs done and who's doing it.

Please, inside, I think, because it's so hot that I'd even rather mop and clean than collect carts and pick up trash, or worse, help unload delivery trucks. I usually get Restock because I'm able to reach the top shelves. On a hot day, like today, it's the best because it's inside. And I can even get a little cold handling the ice cream and frozen foods.

Doggone! Bagging. Well, that's mostly inside. Register B. That's with Sarah, and she's okay.

I run my finger down the list to find Jimmy. No Restock

for him. Not since the Sweet Pickle Catastrophe.

There's his name! Oh, he'll be complaining, for sure: Carts and Parking Lot.

Even on the best days, those're bad. There are four racks in different parts of the lot, but people leave the carts wherever they want, even if the rack is two steps away. When I collect carts, I can't help but think about all the people who are making my job harder by being lazy. GeeGeema says that if you're taking care of lazy people, you'll always be busy. I smile. I wonder if Preston-Cat counts.

Parking Lot is even worse. Mr. Amolsch, the boss, wants no garbage in the lot. None. Everything, every scrap of paper, even the dirty disposable diapers people have the nerve to leave behind have to be picked up and put in the trash cans. And the cans have to be emptied twice a day. On hot days, they stink and there are yellow jackets flying around. The only good thing about it is you get to keep any change you find.

I sign my timesheet and write when I arrived, then put my red-and-white apron on over my blue shirt. I can wear any blue shirt so long as it has at least short sleeves and no writing on it, and any pair of jeans that don't have holes in them. Like Mr. Amolsch says, "If somebody wants to see your skin and your armpits, you should probably run the other way."

Mr. Amolsch is big. Taller than me and big-big-big around. If his beard and hair were white, he'd make a great Santa. He goes out behind the building to smoke at least once every couple of hours, so he always smells of cigarettes. He also drinks three big bottles of cola every day, and not the decaf, diet stuff. He's always joking, in a dad sort of way, even though I don't think he has any kids. To be honest, he isn't dumb. He likes things done right, is all.

Walking to the front of the store, I pass Angel who lucked out and got Restock. She's short and has to use a little ladder to reach the high spots.

"Hey, Angel. Wanna trade?"

She flips her red ponytail. "You wish, Bagger!" When she smiles it's all teeth.

I smile back and adjust so my gums don't show. My hair isn't long enough for a ponytail, yet. Mr. Amolsch doesn't mind it being a little shaggy, so long as it doesn't hang over the eyes.

Then, "You get your phone, yet?"

"No. Next month. Since it got wet, we can't upgrade it. We have to get a new one and that's extra."

Angel gives me a look of pity. "What's it like without it?"

"It's killing me."

At the front, Sarah's been working alone at her register this morning, so she's happy to see me. It's busy, so she just nods and keeps ringing. We don't talk much, even when it's slow. Well, she talks. I listen.

It took a while to get good enough to keep up with her on the register—she's fast. But there are tricks to good bagging, and when the person on the register rings in the right order, it makes things even easier: Heavies together. Colds together. Breakables together. Crushables together. Sarah was a bagger. She knows all the tricks.

But not everybody's good at bagging. Jimmy's fast but isn't careful. I think I'm faster by being more careful, but he'd never agree. Everyone is faster than Angel. I smile. She slows things down so much that Sarah won't let her near her station.

Jimmy rolls in, pushing a long train of carts. He has his blond hair in a ponytail high on the back of his head, so it stays off his neck, but he's still sweaty. When he sees me, he widens his eyes, sticks out his tongue, and drags his feet as if he's dying from the heat. He always makes me smile.

"Hey, Kaz!"

"Hey, Jimmy. Hot?"

"Melting. Found a dollar, though."

"A penny for every degree! But it's supposed to get hotter."

An eye-roll. "Wow, thanks, Kazabee—" His nickname for me. "I feel way better now." The carts bang as he shoves them into their slot. He walks past Sarah and me, toward the back of the store. "Gotta get some water."

Mr. Amolsch doesn't mind a break every once in a while, especially when the weather's hot, but they better not be too often, and they better be short.

*

SK'DOO

"To be or not to be... I know the whole thing!"

"Why can't you just shut the hell up?"

"It's my fault they left. How could anyone ever love me?"

The burial is over.

I used to be among any group of Quicks, listening and learning. That stopped with the lightning-boxes. I miss being with them, but I don't do things that hurt.

I also miss listening to the Dead when they're put in the ground because sometimes they start talking right away. And I might also learn something about the Dead from what the Quick say and feel.

It took a while for me to know that Quicks don't need agreement between what they say, feel, and do. They can be happy that a Quick is now Dead but talk as if it's bad. Or feel sad but act as if nothing at all has happened.

"You're gonna put that where?"

Deads can't act, and as far as I can tell they don't feel anything. At all. I'm not sure, but I think they're always honest. I know I've never had the Dead change what they tell me.

*

KAZ

Ms. Collins comes through the register on her weekly run. She was my grade school librarian but is retired now. She has a bad knee and always asks me to carry her groceries out to her car. Then, she'll give me a quarter even though I tell her I don't want it.

She buys the same things almost every week. A bag of whatever apples are on sale, two large potatoes, a loaf of wheat bread, a pound of ground round, a quart of blue milk, a can of black olives, some fresh vegetables, and two pints of ice cream: vanilla and double-chocolate fudge. This week, she's added small jars of peanut butter and sweet pickles— both are store brand.

I could fit her groceries into two bags, but she always wants four to make them easier to carry when she gets home.

"Four bags, please, dear."

"Yes, Ms. Collins."

"Could you help me carry it out to the car?"

"Yes, Ms. Collins."

At the register, Sarah gives me a wink and a nod.

I lift the bags and walk slowly behind Ms. Collins. I see Jimmy at the far end of the lot, making another cart run.

"I wish I was young and strong like you!"

She always says the same things too.

"You reading any good books this summer?"

"A couple," I lie, hoping she doesn't ask about them.

"I'm glad you started reading. You didn't come into the library that often when you were in elementary school, you know."

I wonder if every librarian remembers everyone who used to visit along with every book they read. For me, dyslexia made the library a confusing place.

Despite her trouble walking, Ms. Collins never parks in one of the handicap spots. Her blue SUV is always down the lot, a row beyond the first cart rack.

"Watch this," she says, as she pulls the car's remote from the bright-yellow pouch she wears around her middle. She fumbles a bit, then stops, straightens her right arm, points the remote at the car, and pushes a button. After a moment, the car *bings* a couple times and the back hatch slowly lifts. She smiles at me. "Magic. I never get tired of that!"

I smile back. She says that every week too. I load the bags into the back of the vehicle.

"Hold on a moment." She unzips another pouch pocket.

"Really, Ms. Collins, you don't have to..."

"No, dear," she says firmly, not looking up from her search for the quarter I know is coming. "You did a little extra work and so you deserve a little extra pay. Never be afraid to accept payment for your work. Remember that."

A sudden, hot breeze blows her grocery receipt from one of the bags and around the side of her car.

"I'll get that!" I say.

Jimmy appears from behind us, as if out of nowhere. "Too slow, Kazabee!" He dashes between the SUV and the cart rack, head down, grabbing for the slip of paper bouncing along the ground, out into the lane beyond.

He runs right in front of the car. It's not moving fast and is one of those new ones with automatic everything. It slams on its brakes, but it's still too late. There's a thud when the car hits Jimmy and a loud crack when his head hits the blacktop.

I don't remember much right after the accident. I run into the store, yelling. Somebody calls emergency. I go back out to the lot. Together, Ms. Collins and I watch as the car's driver checks Jimmy. I see that his hair is dark with blood but when I try to move closer, the driver holds up a hand and orders me to stay back.

It only takes a couple minutes for the cops to show up. A couple minutes after, the fire truck and ambulance arrive. Almost right away, they put Jimmy on a stretcher, cover him with a blanket, and roll him in the back. When they take off without a siren, I know I'll never hear anybody call me Kazabee again.

*

MAZIE

Two cops. "Girly" and "Studly."

Girly's about my height; Studly's a little taller. Both are good-looking in that well-groomed-tight-black-uniform sort of way. Her figure is obscured by her body armor and the gear she carries around her waist.

Studly is another story. Definitely a V-shaped alpha who has himself some muscles. He's flexing as many of them as possible with every word he writes.

They ran my license, and I am sure found it to be perfectly clean. No tickets, no warnings, no accidents, no incidents, at least up until this point in my driving career. Now, to be expected, it's twenty-questions time. Both are taking notes. Girly has my license, snapped to her clipboard.

She's in charge, standing back a little, making Studly do all the work. I suppress a smile as I wonder what he thinks of having a butch-bleach-blonde female order him around. Probably adores it, but I bet that's not what he tells the other boys.

Girly's sunglasses remain in place. His are up on his forehead, showing sky-blue eyes, which combined with short dark hair, dusky complexion, a small neat dark mustache, and very white, very straight teeth make him relatively attractive.

Too bad he's a cop.

I try to hide my disdain for authority but my attempt lacks the perfection of my driving record. The humidity and blast furnace heat rolling up from the asphalt are not helping.

"No, officers, I didn't see him. He wasn't there, then he was. He dashed from behind the vehicle and directly into my path. No, he did not look for traffic. Ask them." I jerk a thumb toward the two other witnesses standing some distance away. "They saw the whole thing."

"Yes, ma'am. They'll be interviewed. We need to get your statement, first." Then, in response to me turning away, he tilts his head. "You having some trouble, ma'am?"

I look at the ground and put my hand up to shade my eyes. "The lights, from the fire truck and your cars. It's disconcerting."

"They take a little getting used to," Studly says. He surprises me by stepping around, with Girly following, so I can turn my back on the lights. It helps. A little.

I smile at him. "Thank you."

He smiles back, a glimmer of humanity. "No problem." Then, it's right back to business. "Did you hit the brakes?"

"No. The car beat me to it."

"How fast would you say you were traveling?"

"I don't know—parking lot speed, I suppose. I'm sure the car keeps track of that, why don't you check it?"

I must've come off a little flippant because both cops look up from their notebooks and harden their attitudes. Here we go.

Girly speaks up. Her wonderfully commanding voice is a notch too high for my taste. "Ma'am? You do understand that a boy died? After being struck by the vehicle you were driving?"

They're statements but she asks like they're questions. I despise that.

"We can either do this our way, or we can call for a tow, impound your vehicle, go over it with a fine-toothed comb, and return it in, oh, say, four weeks? Maybe?"

I can see my frustrated self in her sunglasses, lights flashing behind me.

She raises her right eyebrow. "Your choice?"

I look her right in my reflection. I suppose this stud-cop, bitch-cop routine's supposed to disarm and intimidate me. *Idiots. Think you're in charge.* If you knew what I do to children like that sad-but-pretty little piece of fluff over there in the apron, you'd forget all about this idiot kid who stupidly killed himself by running in front of my car. Our conversation would not center on my parking lot driving speed.

"Yes. I know he died," I say sharply. "I remember, quite distinctly, seeing his brains through his cracked skull." Then I pretend to surrender, sighing, slouching, rubbing my brow, and shaking my head. "I'm sorry, this is a new experience for me. Please. Ask your questions."

In the back of my mind, I'm thinking this damned chunky dude better not've scuffed my car's front bumper. But the biggest kick in the ass is that this is the first time I've shopped here. The only reason I stopped was because it was on the way home from the cemetery. All this for a lousy jar of sweet pickles!

*

KAZ

As the fire truck started washing Jimmy's blood from the

parking lot, the police took me home and we talked in front of Mom and Dad. I thought they'd faint when the police pulled into the drive with me in the back seat, where there were no door handles. The neighbors probably now think I'm a criminal, on top of everything else.

Dad drove over and picked up my bike after that.

Chapter Two

KAZ

I'm exhausted. Hardly slept last night.

Every time I close my eyes, I see Jimmy hitting the pavement. Mom wanted to stay home but I told her to go to work and that I'd be fine, but all I've managed to do this morning is get dressed, lay in bed, and cry.

There's a whisper of a knock at my bedroom door.

"Baby? It's GeeGeema."

"Please, GeeGeema, I don't want to talk."

"I don't want to talk, neither, but Preston's telling me it's lunchtime. I can't find the food, and I'm afraid I'll make a mess."

Like it would kill that cat to miss a meal. I sigh. "Okay. Be right out." I wipe my eyes, blow my nose, toss the tissue on the growing pile beside my bed, and open my door.

"Ha!" GeeGeema grabs my wrist with a surprisingly strong grip. "Gotcha now."

I'm bigger than her, but she pulls me back into my tiny room, sits on my messy bed, and yanks me down beside her.

"Ouch! GeeGeema... Let go!"

"Only if you promise me not to run away. Old days, I'd catch you up. Now, I'm not so fast anymore. Promise now." She bends my wrist. "No running!"

"Ow! I promise. No running."

"No walking fast neither." She smiles, applying more pressure.

"Cut it out, GeeGeema. Let go!" When she does, I rub my wrist. "That hurts! Where'd you learn to do that?"

She laughs and waves a hand at me. "Child, I got talents I ain't even used yet."

The room gets quiet.

"Kaz." She hardly ever calls me that. "Kaz, you have to talk out some of what you're holding in. You keep it inside and it'll make you sick."

"I have to feed Preston first."

"Nope. He's sleeping."

"You lied to me to get me to open my door!"

Again, she laughs. "I lie all the time but nobody listens enough to catch me. Or maybe all y'all just think I'm addled. But whatever, Preston is fast asleep and you still have to talk."

"I don't know what to say."

"Then listen." GeeGeema takes a deep breath. "I know you've been in here, crying over your friend, and that's a fine thing to do, but you're not the first person to lose a friend, you know. I lost one too, when I was younger than you. A boy name of Kenny."

"Kenny?"

"Yes. Kenny. A bunch of us were swimming in the river near home, where I grew up. He was a farm boy. Tall, strong, and fast. Honest. Sang in the church choir. Good swimmer. Almost as good as me. Fine-looking too, especially when we were in swimming, dark skin, all wet and shiny."

"GeeGeema—eww!"

She smiles, but she's gazing past me, her almost blind eyes bright. "I challenged him to a race across the river. Wasn't that far. We both dove in. I made it to the other side and was hollering up a storm because I was first. But..." She shakes her head.

"Kenny didn't make it?"

GeeGeema looks off to the side, away from me. "No. The men found him on the bottom caught up in a snag. He dove too deep, got tangled, and drown. Nobody ever said anything to me about it being my fault, but I always figured that if I hadn't made him race, Kenny wouldn't have drowned. And he'd've grown to be a fine, strong man and..."

It breaks my heart to see her so sad. I take her hands, crying a little at her pain. "But GeeGeema, it wasn't your fault! You didn't make him dive that deep. You didn't know there was something in the water. If you knew he was in trouble, you would've saved him. I know you. You would've done everything you could!"

"Bless you for thinking of me that way, and I know that's true, but, even after all these years, I still feel badly over it. There are some things even Old Father Time can't erase." She hands me the tattered tissue she always keeps up her left sleeve. "Here, now, dry your eyes and wipe your nose."

I do, smelling old lady. "I know what you're telling me. That I could've never known the wind was going to blow Ms. Collins' receipt from her grocery bag."

"That's right."

"No way I could've stopped Jimmy from chasing after that stupid piece of paper. He would've never've listened. He would've laughed. He always had to be faster than me. And he was never careful!" I look at GeeGeema. "He died from being who he was."

She nods back. "That's what most people do."

"I still feel bad about it."

"You always will. Just like any other good person."

I give her a hug.

She holds on to me. "People die because they live. One goes with the other. If you're blessed with a long life, you'll say so many goodbyes to those you love. It's part of the price you pay for growing old." She lets me loose.

"Like you?"

"Yes. Not only Kenny, but my brothers, my parents, your Uncle Gussie, your great-granddaddy, your granddaddy, your gramma. More friends than I care to count. I miss them all. But it's important not to hold such things inside yourself. That never helps anybody. Understand?"

"I think so."

"Good!" She rubs her hands together. "Now you help this old lady off this bed so we can see if my pretty boy is up and about. It's well past his lunchtime."

I help her stand. She doesn't seem so fragile anymore.

"GeeGeema, can you show me how to do that wrist thing?"

"Happy to, but first, let's feed Preston, and get us some eats. After that, I want you to make your bed, and for the Lord's sake, pick up and throw away all those snot rags in your room. It's plain unsanitary, letting those things lay around like that!"

*

SK'DOO

"The same guy who named his pit bull God."

"Mine too, must be the salt water."

"Drop your rosary, Charlie, our prayers have been answered."

Another grave being dug. This one in Rise, near Ottmar, the Oak. My trees are my oldest friends. All the big ones have names. Ottmar in Rise. Silas the Sycamore in Damps. Amy the Hickory in Flats. Lyman the Walnut in Potters Field. And Elba the Butternut. She's the tallest, up on Hill. I climb her, sometimes, and it seems I can see all the way to always.

"Those keys... I can never find those goddam keys!"

I think of them as my trees because I whispered in the ears of all the caretakers who planted them. I wanted all of them to make some sort of food for the squirrels.

Squirrels follow me wherever I go. They don't last long, but they have a good time. I sometimes zoom along with them, fast as can be, along the ground, over the stones, and up the trees. If I could be anything besides me, I'd be a squirrel. Running and scolding like they do. Always brave. Always causing trouble. I wonder what it's like to have a tail?

"I love you more than life."

I've not been able to get any squirrel-feeding trees planted since the lightning-boxes. I can't get close enough to the caretaker to whisper so I hope the trees I have last a long time.

In my memory, no adult Quicks have actually heard my whispers. But some get the idea of what I'm telling them, like Young No Hands who even seems to know when I'm near.

When a Quick is here looking for a Dead, but doesn't know where they are, I can lead them right to the place, if they pay attention. I can whisper, but I have other tricks that work better. My favorite is blowing puffs of air in their faces. Or tickling their earlobes. Or slowing one foot. I can do all those things and others, as long as there are no lightning-boxes.

"That'll never flush."

Babies know I'm here; they look at me and wave their tiny arms and kick their tiny legs. Some very small children too, and we sometimes play hide-and-seek around the stones. That goes away when they start to talk.

Dogs often sit when I am near. Cats stare, but none let me get too close. Animals who wander through make big circles to avoid me, except deer. They stand and stare and stare and stare, then run.

Long in the past, I learned that when some things are close, I can see what they see.

It first happened while watching a singing frog on a tree. It didn't see me, so I looked closer and closer until, suddenly, I saw what the frog saw. I un-frogged as quickly as I could because I didn't want to be a frog. I slowly came to know that I could frog, and un-frog, whenever I wanted. But being a frog is mostly about finding another frog and making more frogs. That's worse than listening to Deads!

"Daddy shouldn't touch me like that."

Calmer than frogs are toads. With toads, I learned what it was to sit and sleep. The strangest thing about toads is that even the smallest ones think they're big and important.

Birds don't see me, so I tried them, thinking I'd fly with a bird, go over Edge, and see other places. I did fly, but Edge goes up into the sky. How far, I don't know, but at least as high as a bird flies. I was lightninged and found myself near Lyman in Potters Field.

I was never a bird again because I don't do things that hurt.

I've been a baby bird. That's when I learned hunger and eating, but that's all they feel and do. Deads are more interesting.

I was a chipmunk, once. It zings me to be one, though

the chipmunk didn't mind. But being chipmunk isn't worth the zing because all chipmunks do, besides worry about finding enough food, is worry about being eaten, worry about being too far from home, worry about where they're going to hide, and worry about what will happen if they meet another chipmunk.

Most things that know I'm here either won't hold still, like squirrels, or won't let me get close, like cats. But dogs trust me, so I tried one of them, once. It hurt me like Edge. It hurt the dog too. And I don't do things that hurt.

I've not tried it with a Quick and never will. It seems the smarter the thing, the more it hurts and Quicks are smarter than dogs. I think. Maybe. I suppose. Though if I had to choose between the two, I'd be a dog. After being a squirrel.

"Run, run, as fast as you can..."

Chapter Three

KAZ

I'm not brave enough to go to Jimmy's funeral service, but I do "pay my respects" like GeeGeema said I should.

I almost turn around when I see the long line. But I stick it out because I figure Jimmy would come see me. There are so many of us, they need two books for signatures. All of his friends and other kids from school are here, but nobody says hi, except Angel, from the store. I understand when she doesn't stay with me.

There's a board with pictures starting from when he was a baby. I'm okay until I see the one with him in a blue T-shirt and red-and-white apron. His goofy smile makes me start to cry, but everyone is crying. Even Mr. Amolsch.

There's an old, old person in front of me in the line who slips a dollar into a fold of cloth in the casket. They catch my eye, give a sad smile, and say, "For the Ferryman."

I'll have to look up what that means. Maybe GeeGeema knows.

I've seen dead people before but Jimmy's the first my age. He looks like he's asleep, but not really, because he also looks like he's held in place, somehow. He's in regular clothes. That's good because I don't think any of us have ever seen him in a suit. They have his hair combed which makes him look different.

Jimmy's parents look plain wore out. I don't want to talk to them because they look like they've already talked to too many people, but I introduce myself, to be polite.

When I tell them my name, they say Jimmy had mentioned me when he talked about work and school. That he said I was a good friend. I know they're being nice, but the good friend thing restarts my crying.

When I leave, Mr. Amolsch is outside. Blowing the smoke out the side of his mouth, he asks me how I'm doing and if I'll be able to come back to the store because he'd hate to lose such a good worker. I tell him I will, in a couple more days. He surprises me with a big hug—like a hug from a mountain—and says I'm brave.

I don't feel that way.

*

The burial, which is the only part that I sort of want to see, is family only. But they tell me where the grave will be; near the big oak tree in the middle of Eastdale.

A couple of hours later, I take my bike to the cemetery and ride on the outside road to be sure everyone from his family is gone. It's easy to find the grave because there's only one really big oak in the place. The roads in the middle of the cemetery are gravel, making it harder to pedal. Once I'm near, I lay my bike on the ground. I figure there's nobody around to steal it.

A bunch of squirrels run away from me as I walk to Jimmy's grave. It's on the little rise toward the hill, just up from the tree. His family has been in town a long time, so there are other people with his last name all around him. That's nice, I guess.

I wasn't sure what I thought I'd see. What's here is a rectangular pile of fresh dirt with heat-wilted flowers on top. There isn't any stone for him. I never thought about it, but I suppose those take a while. There is a plastic sign that says, "We Love You." Looking at that, I almost start to cry. Almost. I'm getting better.

I stand, hands together in front of me. I'm not from a family that prays. GeeGeema says it's best to say what you need to right to the person who needs to hear it instead of hoping God delivers the message for you.

"Jimmy, this is Kaz. Kazabee," I say out loud. Then, I stop because it feels dumb to talk to a dead person. What do they have to say back?

*

SK'DOO

"My name is James, but everyone calls me Jimmy."

That's the first thing this new Dead says to me. I wasn't able to be close for the burial, but the gravediggers cleaned up extra fast because it's a day they don't usually work. I moved in as soon as they were gone.

"I don't know what happened. I was There, now I'm Here." That's exactly what Hannah Griggs says. I know that Deads use the same words to mean the same things, so like Hannah, Jimmy must've gone from Quick to Dead in a hurry.

"Kazabee was there when it happened."

"Kazabee?" What's a Kazabee?

"My name is James, but everyone calls me Jimmy."

Ah, repeating. That sometimes happens. Some Deads

never get past the first few things they say. Some tell you more about themselves. But most of them repeat, at least at first.

A Quick with no lightning-box walks from Center Road to stand beside me. It's Young No Hands.

They stand, hands together. "Jimmy, this is Kaz... Kazabee."

Kazabee? That's the name of Young No Hands! How nice to find out the name of a Quick I know so well.

As usual, it is so easy to understand their feelings. I know they want to stay longer but are unsure. They used to sit by Silas, maybe they'll sit here, by Ottmar.

I blow small puffs of air into their eyes until they look over at the nearby bench. I push a little on the back of their head to get things moving in that direction and bump knees to help them sit. I feel Kazabee's deep sorrow and confusion, almost like when they sat with Silas. I decide to stay. Their emotions always match what they think. It's a chance to help and learn.

*

KAZ

My allergies must be acting up with this dust that's getting in my eyes. There's a bench. In the shade. I sigh. It's so nice and quiet. Maybe I'll sit for a little while. Sit and not think.

But I can't not think, looking at Jimmy's grave. I think about him in the ground, right there, right in that spot, where he'll be forever. He'll never grow up. I'll never see his face again. Same as GeeGeema with Kenny. I wipe my eyes with the stupid half-torn tissue I jammed in my back pocket before leaving the house. I feel like I did before, when I was depressed and did nothing but cry.

I relax a little and feel a calm come over me. My breathing slows. I know from my time sitting over by the sycamore that if I'm quiet for a while, the squirrels will start wandering close by. I smile a little. I always like that.

A dark car comes down the gravel road from the hill and stops. A person gets out and starts walking toward me.

*

MAZIE

I figured that since I was visiting my lovely pond creature, I'd stop and see the latest in my series. True, he wasn't intentional. Nothing more than pure, delicious serendipity. I'll admit he wasn't my type. Not that I have anything against boys, I'm an equal opportunity collector, it's just that he was both a bit too Chunky Dude and too old for me. All the same, he was alive until he ran into me. I smile at my little joke.

Remembering that *thud* when my car struck him gives me the same sort of thrill as the chokes and the struggles, even if he did scuff my front bumper. I won't add him to the list since he wasn't intentional. But if I ever did, I would include an asterisk.

I pull down the gravel road from the top of the hill. I'd looked up the family name in the cemetery records and figured he'd be buried somewhere in this area, down near that messy, big-assed tree. And, sure enough, there's a fresh grave. Damn...look at all the squirrels. Good thing they're not predators!

When I'm as close to the grave as I can manage, I stop and exit the car. The gravestones here are newer but smaller than those on the higher ground. In both life and death, the rich and powerful always get the best real estate. Always.

A bike, flat on the ground. I huff. Kids nowadays. Never take care of anything. I see somebody sitting on a bench a couple of dozen steps this side of the grave. A little closer and I realize it's that pretty little piece of fluff from the parking lot. How nice.

Pretty Fluff appears taller than I like, but I'd never hunt her, anyway. We're tied together by Chunky Dude's death. If Fluff turned up missing, my life would be examined at least in some fashion, and the last thing I want is a bunch of cops poking their noses into my business—even if they are idiots. But that doesn't preclude some small amount of fun.

*

SK'DOO

This new Quick has a lightning-box. I move away, making a wide circle to get back to Jimmy the Dead. That's where I really belong.

"Kazabee was there when it happened."
"I'm fast enough to catch that receipt."
"I wonder what's for dinner."

*

KAZ

They have shoulder-length hair: straight, black, banged, and tucked behind their ears. Dressed in black too: not-too-tight jeans, a loose T-shirt, square-toed boots. Must be hot in the sun. They're thin, tall, and tan, but not dark. There's a gold bracelet on their right wrist.

They walk right over to me.

"May I sit down?" A female-sounding voice that's quiet and shy. Not high or low, but in the middle. Nails just to the end of their fingers, red, manicured. They have on lipstick and little bit of eyeliner, but no perfume. A she, probably.

I move to get up to leave, she asks me not to and says she's only staying for a few moments. She sits at the far end of the bench and folds her hands into her lap.

"Did you know him?" she asks, nodding at the grave.

"Yeah. Jimmy was my friend. My good friend, I guess." I glance at her face, and it clicks. "You were driving the car!"

"Oh..." She's surprised. "You were with the old lady!" She looks at the ground, then at me. She's very pretty with her straight nose and mouth that turns down a little. Her eyes are black too. "You told the police there was no way I could've stopped. They said the other witnesses corroborated my statement when they called to say there'd be no charges or investigation." She smiles a little—perfect white teeth with no gums showing. "Thanks for telling the truth."

Her face goes sad. "I've had trouble sleeping since the accident." Her voice cracks a little. "I keep replaying it over and over in my head, trying to think of what I could've done to avoid him." She looks at the ground, at the grave, then back at me. Her eyes are so sad.

"Me too. At first, whenever I closed my eyes all I saw was Jimmy hitting the ground."

"Sounds like we have a lot in common."

"Yeah."

"Too bad what we have in common is what happened to Jimmy." She reaches the distance of the bench and touches the back of my hand. "I'm sorry."

I feel so bad for her. I look her in the eyes. "I know it's not your fault he died. It happened so fast. Nobody could've stopped." For what seems like the millionth time in the last week, tears start to form, but I manage not to cry.

She reaches again, squeezes my hand, and lets go. I can see the muscles in her arm, but they're not big. Her fingers are warm.

She smiles at me. "May I ask your name?"

"Kaz. I'm Kaz Delcorio."

"Well, Kaz Delcorio, I'm Mazie Maddington. I'm very happy we happened to meet."

"Me too, Ms. Maddington."

"Please, call me 'Mazie.' Ms. Maddington makes me feel like an old schoolteacher."

"Okay...Mazie."

"I have a friend up on the hill and I visit fairly often." She tilts her head in that direction. "Ride up that way when you're here. Maybe we'll run into each other some other time."

I nod. "Maybe."

She stands up. "Well, I have to get going. Looks like rain, doesn't it?"

"Yeah. Me too." I point in the direction of her car. "My bike's over there. GeeGeema'll be wondering where I've been."

"'GeeGeema?'"

I feel myself blush a little. "My great-great-gramma. She lives with us. But saying great-great-gramma all the time is a pain, so I shortened it to GeeGeema."

Mazie laughs. "Inventive."

I lean down to pick up my bike. "Not really."

She touches my shoulder. "Don't sell yourself short, Kaz, that's the worst thing a person can do." When she walks over to her car, it unlocks by itself. "I've been thinking about trading it, because of what happened to your friend. What do you think?"

I look down at the front bumper, the one that killed Jimmy. "I...I don't know."

"Neither do I," she says as she sits down. She swings her legs in, gives me a smile and a little wave. "See you later, I hope." She shuts the door. I can't see inside because of the tint. The car pulls away; the only sounds it makes are the tires on the gravel.

*

MAZIE

It looks like Pretty Fluff is in the process of growing out her hair. It's unkempt, but clean, brown, in ringlets, with a wicked cowlick behind the left ear. She's dressed in a plain white, boy's T-shirt, faded, sort of baggy, store-brand boy's jeans, and scuffed running shoes. Though it doesn't look like that particular activity is a favorite. Tall, thin, tawny skin, undefined muscles. Indeterminate age, but late teens from the length of her limbs. No makeup. No jewelry, though her ears are pierced. An androgynous face with a pleasing mix of adult and not-quite-adult features. I like her eyes and mouth, especially. There's potential for great looks. Attractive, especially to me. Excluding height, she would definitely do, were I hunting, which I firmly remind myself I am not.

I know that kids tend to freak when they see me all in black, and it's not what I would've worn had I known we were going to meet. So, I walk over to the bench as meekly as possible. "May I sit down?"

Fluff moves to get up.

I put out a hand. "No. Please don't leave. I'm only going to be here a few moments." I sit at the end of the bench, as far away as possible. I lower my chin toward the fresh grave. "Did you know him?"

"Yeah. Jimmy was my friend. My good friend, I guess."

Her voice is deeper than I expected, sad and resigned, broken. Then recognition dawns. Her big brown eyes widen. "You were driving the car!"

I'm surprised I'm recognized so quickly. Pays at least a little attention to the world. I point a finger at her as if remembering.

"Oh, you were with the old lady!" I look at the ground and back, widening my eyes a bit and talking a little faster than usual, to give the impression of being a bit out of control. "You told the police there was no way I could've stopped." I calm my voice and add gratitude. "They said the other witnesses corroborated my statement when they called to say there'd be no charges or investigation." I smile and wrinkle my nose a little. I know I'm extra cute when I do that. "Thanks for telling the truth."

Now, let's turn on the sad face. "I've had trouble sleeping since the accident." A complete lie, but oh, that voice crack was great! "I keep replaying it over and over in my head, trying to think of what I could've done to avoid him." I look at the ground, the grave, then at Fluff, cranking up the sad.

I see my emotions reflected.

"Me too. At first, whenever I closed my eyes all I saw was Jimmy hitting the ground."

My somber voice. "Sounds like we have a lot in

common."

"Yeah," Fluff replies. So much sorrow in that contralto voice.

"Too bad what we have in common is what happened to Jimmy." I touch the back of her hand. "I'm sorry."

"I know it's not your fault he died. It happened so fast. Nobody could've stopped!" Fluff almost cries.

I imagine she's done little else over the past few days. Overemotional teens are all alike. I take a big chance, reach over, and gently squeeze her hand. Short, clean, filed nails. Not manicured. Her skin is curiously cool for such a warm day. Low blood pressure. Probably suffers from dizziness.

She doesn't pull away or flinch from the touch. Encouraging.

"May I ask your name?"

"Kaz. I'm Kaz Delcorio."

"Well, Kaz Delcorio, I'm Mazie Maddington and I'm very happy we happened to meet." I give a shy look and refrain from smiling too widely.

"Me too, Ms. Maddington."

"Call me Mazie—Ms. Maddington makes me feel like an old schoolteacher."

"Okay...Mazie." She smiles but is clearly uncomfortable calling adults by their given names. Another tool to use.

"I have a friend up on the hill and I visit fairly often." I motion in that direction. "Ride up that way when you're here. Maybe we'll run into each other some other time." She misses the connection between me running into her and me running into Chunky Dude.

"Maybe."

I figure that's enough for today. That'll probably be it. Seeing as I'm only playing and not looking for the next one for my list. I figure she's too shy to take the bait. I smile at her, then stand. "Well, I have to get going. Looks like rain, doesn't it?"

"Yeah. Me too." Kaz-Fluff points in the direction of my car. "My bike's over there. GeeGeema'll be wondering where I've been."

"'GeeGeema?'"

Was that a blush? How wonderful—I adore blushers.

"She's my great-great-gramma. She lives with us. But saying great-great-gramma all the time is a pain, so I shortened it to GeeGeema."

Now, that has got to be one of the dumbest things I've ever heard, but I laugh. "Inventive." I give a stare and smile.

Kaz-Fluff picks up her bicycle. "Not really."

Huh. More self-aware than appearances would dictate, perhaps, or simply teenage angst? I reach out with my right hand and squeeze her left shoulder. Through the T-shirt I feel the solidity of a collarbone beneath a layer of cool, soft flesh. The touch is nearly overwhelming. There's a flash of wrapping my arm around her neck. I tamp the thought down—way down. I consider that my approaching her was a mistake. No...I'm sure I can play. It'll be like that movie, with death, on a holiday.

Serious face. "Don't sell yourself short, Kaz. That's the worst thing a person can do." I walk over to my car and it unlocks itself. I can't resist a last emotional dig. "I've been thinking about trading it, because of what happened to your friend. What do you think?"

She looks at the front bumper. "I...I don't know."

"Neither do I." I get in the car, give a smile and a little wave with just my fingertips. "See you later, I hope."

I know I can't be seen once I shut the door and smile and shiver simultaneously. As I pull away, I'm thinking I deserve a best actor award of some sort and laugh at how easy it is to manipulate this one. This is going to be a crap-ton of fun, that is, if there's a return engagement. I'm leaving that completely up to fate and Kaz-Fluff!

*

SK'DOO

I sit with Dead Jimmy and watch the two Quicks. They seem like strangers, at first. But when they start touching, I'm not sure. I've never been able to figure out the feelings Quicks have for each other because they can say one thing yet feel another. That confuses me.

Every once in a while, I find a Quick like Kazabee and can feel what they feel. But when I can't, I have to guess by the way they move or by the sound of their voices. I've heard enough of them say they're sad, or happy, or angry, or in love to try to match up what they say with the way they act. But I'm not very good at it.

"Crap! I dropped all those sweet pickles!"

I watch Kazabee and the new Quick touch hands and wonder what that's like. In the past Quicks came here, late in the dark, and hugged, kissed, and undressed. I've watched naked Quicks and the silly-looking things they do to each other when they're that way. They seem to enjoy it, mostly, but I don't understand those things. There aren't naked Quicks here at night anymore. They must have stopped doing that.

But I still see kisses and hugs and I know there are different kinds. People at burials kiss and hug differently from people who are walking together. More confusion.

"Yeah, I know, I should be more careful."

It's getting dark, the Quicks are gone from the bench, and I feel lightning growing near. I zoom over to H.H. Haven.

*

KAZ

I hear thunder off in the distance. I watched the forecast with GeeGeema and it said it would stay hot for least another three days. But maybe if it rains, it'll cool down a little.

The house isn't too hot, so long as I don't move around much, but riding my bike from place to place isn't any fun in weather like this. I could drive, but that's a pain because then we have to figure out who needs what car. It's easier to bike, even if I do sweat.

There's a flash of lightning. I use the trick GeeGeema taught me. First, count the seconds after the flash until it thunders then divide by five to get how many miles away it is. Ten seconds makes it two miles.

It starts to rain. Sounds like it's coming down pretty hard.

I keep thinking about Mazie at the cemetery and how sad she was about Jimmy. It was brave of her to visit the grave and nice of her to talk to me. She's easy to talk to. Doesn't rush. Isn't loud. Doesn't tease. I don't think I've ever talked to anybody that pretty, and I know nobody that pretty has ever talked to me.

A flash: one, two, thr—, then a long roll of thunder that rattles the window of my little room. So, like, two-and-a-half. I do the numbers in my head, which dyslexia makes difficult, and come up with five miles, but I know that's wrong because ten was two. I feel my face scrunch as I search for the mistake. Oh. The stupid decimal point. The answer is point-five miles. A half a mile.

The lightning gets so fast I can't tell what thunder goes where, so there's no use counting. The wind blows the rain against the side of the house and I snuggle down into my pillow a little more.

I wonder who Mazie's friend is, buried on the hill. I thought they were all old graves up there. I'll ride out tomorrow to see if I can figure it out. Maybe she'll be there too. I can feel myself blush a little. I hate blushing, maybe even more than showing my gums when I smile.

Flash-*boom*! Yikes—no need to count on that one!

*

SK'DOO

Haven is a perfect name for the marker that sits above this grave. Made of blue metal, it's empty inside, and here I feel no zings from anything, not even lightning.

Until Haven, I hid in tree hollows, then, after it was built, in Stone Vault where, before the digging machines, bodies were stored in the winter when the ground was frozen. I felt plenty of bad lightning-zings when I hid in the trees, and even in Stone Vault. When I'm inside Haven I don't feel or see anything.

Sometimes, it seems that if I stayed long enough, I'd vanish, so I stay out of Haven unless there's a storm. Because were I gone, who would listen to the Dead?

Beneath this marker is Horace Howard Haven who became Quick in 1790 and Dead in 1889. He sometimes says he wishes he would've lived one more year. But sometimes says he is glad he didn't. Neither sounds like a lie. His first wife died because he wouldn't pay for medical care. His second wife killed herself to escape him. He buried both of his wives in Potters Field to save the money for himself. With the amount of time I've known him, I should know more, but H.H. is one of the worst repeaters I listen to. He hardly ever says anything I don't already remember.

I suppose H.H. spent the money he saved on his wives' burials for his own. His is the only big metal marker. And I remember his hearse, the fancy black one, pulled by two horses.

How I miss horses! It used to be, at a big burial, there might be a dozen of them standing, stomping, and tossing their heads. I spent almost as much time around them as I did the Quicks and knew some of them as well as the Deads.

When I rode between teams it was as if we were one

thing, all working together, especially when delivering big markers. I remember Bill and Bert, Lily and Tiny, and Becky and Fred.

Like Quicks (and dogs), each grew strong then faded away. Like dogs (but not Quicks), I could trust the way they felt. If a Quick misses a Dead, it can mean many things. But if a horse missed a Quick, it meant it missed a friend.

It's been so long since I've seen a horse, I wonder if there are any left.

I hear a *boom* from the storm outside. I'm glad I'm in Haven!

Chapter Four

KAZ

The forecast was right. Hot and humid. Again.

I give GeeGeema her morning hug.

"I think I see a blue shirt! You going to work today?"

"Yes. I promised Mr. Amolsch I would."

"That's a good thing. Get back into your life."

"I'm not looking forward to being there."

"You think Jimmy would want you moping around and missing out on being alive?"

"No. But I'm still not looking forward to going. I'm afraid I'll start crying again, and I'm sick and tired of crying!"

GeeGeema smiles. "That's my hard-headed baby, right there. I bet you have just a little more crying to do, and you'll be fine."

"I sure hope you're right."

I open a green can of stinky-chicken for Preston, who appears when he hears the sound. "Hey, Fat-Cat."

I take a coffee cup of water and place it in the center of the table. "That was some storm last night, huh?"

"Storm?"

"GeeGeema... Thunder shook the whole house."

"Musta missed it."

"Don't see how."

"Then you don't see everything." She looks at me, sideways. "Anything else happening?"

I think of mentioning Mazie. "Not really."

"Come give me a hug and then haul yourself to work. You be careful. Do good once you get there."

"Yes, GeeGeema. Bye-bye."

"And I love you too!"

*

SK'DOO

"Cleveland would win except for all those lousy calls."

"She can't cook worth a hoot, but she's great in the sack."

"Put the coal to her, Gerard, there's a grade coming up!"

There must have been plenty of wind last night, with all the small tree limbs and leaves all over. The caretaker will probably be early. They always are the day after bad weather, sometimes even before Lady Runner.

*

KAZ

I don't want to be at the store and almost turn around and ride home when I don't see Jimmy's bike at the back of the building. I can feel tears behind my eyes, but park my bike, take a deep breath, and go in through the side door.

There's a new job sheet on the wall. No mention of Jimmy. I don't know whether that makes me happy, sad, or mad. I'm a Bagger, again, and with Sarah, again, just like that day.

I'm aware of something large behind me. I turn, and sure enough, it's Mr. Amolsch.

"I'm glad you made it in, Kaz."

"Thanks."

He pats my shoulder, twice, with a gentle touch for such

a big hand. "It'll be a little rough, but things'll get better from here."

"I sure hope so."

"Trust me."

I put on my apron, take another deep breath, and walk out to the front of the store. Sarah stops ringing, leans in close.

"You cool, kid?" Barely over a whisper, I feel her breath on my neck and get goose bumps.

I nod.

"Good. Let's just keep as busy as we can. Yes?"

"Yes. Busy."

She points to the front windows, out at the parking lot. "I figure that oughta cheer you up."

I look and see Angel, red ponytail bobbing as she collects carts.

"Wow! Look at that."

"She's surprisingly good at it too. Don't have to be too fast." Sarah smirks a little. "I've been dropping extra change in the parking lot all week. Y'know, to encourage her."

I look at Sarah who tilts her head and smiles.

I bust out laughing.

"It's good to have you back, Kaz."

"Yeah. I guess, maybe, it's good to be back."

Things are a little rough when Ms. Collins comes

through on her weekly run. She gives me an old lady hug, and there are some tears, but only a couple. As we walk out with her four bags, I realize she's parked on the other side of the lot.

She sees my look. "I can't park where I used to. You know."

"Yeah. I know."

As I put the bags in her car, she's suddenly angry. "And if that goddamned receipt blows away, you just let it go, you hear me?" Then, there's a pause and she says softly, "I am so sorry for what happened. It's all I've thought about."

I hug her, then let her go. "No, Ms. Collins. Don't you feel bad. You and I, we didn't have anything to do with it. Jimmy died because he was being Jimmy, and that's all there is to it."

She looks at me as if she's never seen me before. "You're very smart, do you know that, dear?"

"I'm not so sure, Ms. Collins."

"Well, I am." She climbs into the front seat and puts out her hand. "Here's your little extra."

I take the money and she drives off.

I'm expecting a quarter so am surprised to find a dollar in change. I put twenty-five cents in my pocket and drop the rest. Seventy-five cents is a small price to pay to keep me off Carts and Parking Lot.

As I return to my station, I'm hit with the idea that maybe Mr. Amolsch and Sarah have been putting money out here all along!

*

SK'DOO

"My teeth hurt when I chew."

"I pray that at least one of my babies will live."

"I like it from behind."

While going to visit Dead Jimmy, I see that Ottmar has lost a branch in last night's storm. It's not big, and he'll be fine, but I don't like to see any of my friends hurt.

So, then, I suppose I should check the others, and while I'm at it, make a round of Edge too. I like doing that because it's quiet, except for the Dead at its corners.

I go down the hill and across Damps to give the one side of Silas I can see a good look. All there, except for a whole mess of his bark that blew off in the wind. Silas does that all the time and I often wonder how he doesn't run out of the stuff.

At the corner of Damps is P.K. Descher. His first name is Park, but everyone called him "Pap." He became Quick in 1899 and Dead in 1977. All the kids loved him, and when he cut the grass, they came to ride in a cart behind his machine.

He bought walnuts and butternuts the boys brought him for five cents a bag, so they'd have some spending money but threw the nuts away because he had no use for them. Sometimes, when he was tired of all the children, he told his wife to say he was taking a nap.

I wait a moment. I always do.

"You dropped a silver dollar into the back porch steps?"

Following Outside Road, I go to a little triangle of ground between Damps and Flat. That's Haven.

I pause, not so much to listen to H.H., but to see if any Quicks are golfing.

What was once covered with trees is now golf, surrounding the Deads and me. I watch and listen all the time, Quicks using bent sticks to hit little balls. Even at this distance, through Edge, I know golf makes Quicks feel one of two ways: happy or angry. Mostly, it's angry. Very angry. Who can understand that?

Across, at the corner of Flats, is Devon Oberlee Sanchez.

"They have all built a shrine to my past."

Devon says they were born on an island called Puerto Rico, and moved here when they were young. They struggled with the strict religion of their parents and the opinions of others because they were thought of as different. Devon loved cats, books, and sharing poetry, but that wasn't enough. One warm, bright day, overwhelmed by loneliness, they took enough medicine to sleep their way to Dead. Devon hasn't been here very long but I'm sure White Beard Old Man knows them. He always slows on his daily walk and sometimes puts a pebble on the grave marker, saying, "One day the sun admitted, I am just a shadow." Often, he cries.

Many Deads tell me they made themselves that way. It doesn't surprise me since I've always known Quicks like Kazabee, sad and by themselves. Not being Dead must be difficult.

From Sanchez, I go clear across Flats and Potters Field, checking that Amy hasn't lost any branches. I can see Sexton's and Caretaker's, but they are on the other side of Edge. Even if I could reach them, I wouldn't go near because of the lightning they hold.

Of all the places I can go, I like Potters Field the best. There are no markers and everything is open and clear. Quicks like Potters Field the least because it's where almost all of them are lost. But I know everyone here, from one corner to the next, and can steer any Quick right to the place they need, as long as there are no lightning-boxes.

It upsets Quicks if they can't find the spot that holds the Dead they're looking for. What the Quicks don't understand is that the Dead don't care if they're visited. Not at all.

At the very, very outside corner of Potters Field is Olive

Mae Wilson. I have no idea what she did to be so far away from everybody else, but here she is, all on her own. It's a good thing Deads never get lonely because if they could, Olive Mae certainly would. The only thing she's ever told me is her name. Once. I know she became Dead in 1875 because I remember others buried when she was. Maybe she talks when she's alone. Maybe she has nothing to say. Maybe there's nothing to tell. Too many maybes.

I move away from Olive Mae toward George Z. Lauffer. She became Quick in 1924 and Dead in 1945 and caused plenty of mischief when she was younger. After some real trouble, she was given the choice between spending her time in jail or going to war. She became Dead when she threw herself onto a grenade to save those around her. The last thing she remembers as a Quick is laughing and says that moving to Dead is walking in a warm rain.

"Another drink? Sure! Why not?"

From G.Z., it's a turn and I go up Hill to Ezme Evans. I look closely at Lyman as I go and see a few small branches down.

Only Elba to check. She's right by Ezme.

For someone who became Dead so young, Ezme has much to say. Hardly any is repeated, and she always surprises me with something new. None of what she says seems very important, but all of it is interesting so I'm looking forward to sitting with her.

When I reach Ezme's grave, I realize something's changed. I should barely be able to get around her stone, but Edge is moved. Instead of dropping down Rise, across Damps, and back to Descher, Edge swings down the back side of Hill toward Pond.

I am unsure what to do. This is...confusing.

Edge hasn't moved since Lauffer was buried. This is new-new. I go back to just before Edge reaches Ezme and follow it along, not too close. I don't do things that hurt.

There! Right at Ezme, it turns away from its usual path.

I go down the far side of Hill. I've never been here. The ground is so tilted! I come to Pond who I've only ever seen from up high on the road. Pond looks so different. Bigger.

Now what?

To follow Edge, I have to go out on Pond. I've traveled over puddles before, but they weren't deep, like Pond. I am...afraid. I've looked at Pond so many times, wanting to get close. Now, I have what I want, and I'm afraid?

Slowly I go out and onto the water. I feel things below. Fast things. Squirrel- and bird-fast, but in the water. Other things too, that are slow. I don't know any of them. New-new.

Once I'm sure I'm going to be on Pond, not in it, I move farther out and feel Edge. I follow back until I reach the corner of Edge coming down from Ezme. It's where water goes when it rains and Pond gets too full.

I'm not sure what to think when I hear, *"Those are so pretty."*

There's a Dead in the water of Pond! I stop. Of course there's a Dead here, or Edge wouldn't be here, would it?

Too much is new-new. I cross back over the water, go up Hill, and stay near Ezme who I know so well.

"A baby came out of Momma and it is a mess!"

I'm still here but have to leave when a black machine comes up Hill and stops. The dark-haired lady from yesterday, Mazie, the one who talked with Kazabee, gets out, crosses the road to the bench, and sits, looking out over Pond and into the woods. I would like to get closer, but she has a lightning-box.

I'll go back to Descher and follow new Edge from there.

*

KAZ

I hurry home from work to change before riding out to the cemetery. I worry about GeeGeema asking questions, but she's napping. I sort of clean up a little, wash my face, and put on extra deodorant in case I smell. Brush my teeth. I feel a little stupid, putting on a black tee. It's not like I want to dress like my crush, or anything. The black shirt was on the top of the pile in the drawer, except it was really the next one down. I don't even bother with my hair, I mean, really. I practice no-gum smiling a couple of times, then hop on my bike.

I don't know who Mazie is exactly, yet. I know she's older than me, but it's okay to have older friends. It would be okay for me to have *any* friends. She's nice and polite. And pretty. I feel myself blush a little and wish, again, I wouldn't do that.

I take the outside road at Eastdale because I can ride faster on it than in the gravel. *Please be there. Please be there. Please be there.* As I round the bend and go up the hill, I see her standing near the bench overlooking the turtle pond.

*

MAZIE

I feel like a fool sitting here, like some adolescent kissy-face waiting for her equally adolescent crush. But it's exactly what I'm doing. I always grow a little crazy at this stage of the process. Thing is, I keep reminding myself, I'm not in any process. Kaz-Fluff is not for my list.

I don't yet know what the teen is to me, precisely. A very

attractive toy, at least. An object to be twisted and squeezed, for fun, then tossed before she figures out what I'm doing.

She's socially inept. Can barely stand to look me in the eye. Extremely shy, at least. On the spectrum, perhaps. Maybe I can pay her back for her troubles by teaching her a little about getting by in the world. Tit for tat, so to speak. I smile.

If she shows, there will be another couple of meetings and that'll be that. Done. Finished. I promise myself. And I'm always very serious about keeping promises—especially the ones I make to me.

I've traded my preferred black attire for something matching that of my potential plaything. A plain white tee and jeans. I even dug out a pair of slightly scuffed runners from the back of my closet. I don't like how big they make my feet look. I pulled my hair back into a ponytail. Makes me look younger. More approachable. Safer.

It's hot, even with the clouds and breeze. I've been sitting for almost an hour, having spent about half meditating on my pond creature and the other half meditating on how long I should wait for Fluff. It's not often I can delight in arranging circumstances so my next target unknowingly spends time near my last—except, I remind myself again, Fluff is not my next target.

I've suddenly had enough. "This is bullshit!" I say out

loud. I stand, look at the pond one last time, and turn to walk to my car. I haven't taken a step when a familiar face rides up the hill.

*

KAZ

I wave. I'm disappointed to see she's wearing a white tee. Now, I feel even more stupid.

"Hey, Mazie! I was hoping you were here!"

"Just got here myself. We must have a psychic connection!"

I smile, remembering to hide my gums, and lean the bike against the end of the bench. "Can we sit instead of walk?"

"Sure! Sit. I was just going to do that."

I plunk myself down. Not too close because I'm sweaty and might stink.

"The wind sure feels good," I start. "You wore a white shirt."

"And you wore a black one!"

I blush.

Mazie smiles, then rubs the side of her face. "We both thought we'd be twins but ended up being each other."

"I guess so. I feel kind of dumb now."

"Well, if you're dumb, then so am I. Tell you what. How about, from now on, we dress the way we want. You know, be who we really are."

I nod, even though I'm pretty sure she doesn't want to know who I really am.

"I'm more comfortable in black. And with your color, you look much better in white. You think?"

I'm not used to people mentioning color, but she's right, I look better in white than black.

Mazie suddenly gets this crazy look on her face. "Hey, Kaz, how about we trade and be who we're supposed to be?"

"Trade?"

"Trade shirts." She stands up and looks around. "Come on, the coast is clear."

"*Here*? Are you crazy? Somebody will see!"

She swings her arms. "Check it out! Nobody for miles."

I cannot believe it when she pulls her shirt over her head and holds it out to me.

"Kaz, hurry! If somebody sees me, it'll be all your fault!"

This is crazy! But then I think I can be as brave as she is. I don't stand up, but slide to the edge of the bench, yank my shirt off, and throw it at her. "Here! Gimme mine!"

Once dressed, we start to laugh. I lean against her a little and it seems okay to do that. I think about wearing the shirt she had on.

"Hey, Kaz," she says, smiling.

"Yeah?"

"Your shirt's on backwards."

"Oh, crap." I pull out the collar and see the printing that's supposed to be behind my head. There's no way I'm taking it off again, so I pull my arms inside the shirt and spin it around. "All fixed."

Then, I notice hers and smile back. "But yours is backwards *and* inside out."

"No problem." She glances around. Then, going slower than I would sitting in my own room, pulls her shirt off, turns it right-side out, and puts it back on.

I don't want to stare, but I do. All of her skin is tan. I don't see any lines. She's not very big on top, and is wearing a lacy, white bra. She's in great shape, toned, not like me. I can see her muscles, but they're small and smooth, not big or lumpy. I glance away, then into her face.

She's looking at me with shining black eyes.

"All fixed." She smiles.

I can tell I'm blushing. I'm glad I wasn't caught staring.

"So, Kaz. What gives me the feeling you don't undress in public all that often?"

"I've never undressed in public."

Mazie laughs. "You mean until now!"

I look away, then back at her. I feel myself grinning.

"Yeah. Until now."

She laughs again. "And we managed to do it before that old man with the beard could catch us!"

My smile vanishes. "That would've been bad."

Her eyes sparkle. "Shoot. He hasn't seen anything as good as us in so long, he'd probably faint!" She leans over to push me with her shoulder. "From now on, every time you're here, you can remember the first time you ever got half-naked...in a cemetery."

I smile. No gums!

Then, she turns serious. "You doing better today?"

"Better?"

"Yesterday you were pretty upset."

"A little better. I went back to work."

"Did he work there too?"

I nod.

"That must've been pretty hard."

"It was, at first. But it got easier."

"You two must've been close. Was he your boyfriend?"

My eyes fill up. "Not my boyfriend. It's just..."

"Just what, Kaz?"

"Just that he was the only friend I had."

"Oh, sweetheart." Mazie slides off the bench, gets on her knees in front of me, and holds my hands. Hers are so warm. "You can't mean that. You must have other friends."

"I mean it. He was my only friend. Everyone else..."

"Everyone else...what?"

I'm trying so hard not to cry that I can't talk.

"Everyone else what?" she repeats.

Great. I just met her and I'm telling her this. "You'll think I'm weird."

"Kaz. Nobody is weirder than me. Trust me, girl."

I whisper, "That's just it. I'm not a girl. Not female."

"Not a girl? I'm sorry, Kaz. Are you male?"

I sit back and look at the ground. "No. It's confusing."

"Sure is. Can you tell me? Please? I want to help." She shakes my hands a little. "Please, Kaz, tell me. Just start and let the words come out on their own."

I shake my head. "I can't..." I know what she'll think, but I keep talking. "Jimmy sat with me at lunch. Always talked to me in the hall. Joked and made me smile. He treats me...treated me like I was just plain old me." My voice starts to break. "That's what I liked about him. He didn't care." My emotions come so fast and hard that I can't stop them.

From her knees, Mazie puts her arms around my neck. It feels so good to be held. I hug her back, hard.

She wipes the tears off my face with the tail of her T-shirt. "Now, you sit up here. Look at me, Kaz. Come on, look at me. Listen, I don't quite understand what you're going through, but it's obviously a big deal. Please tell me that you're getting counseling for this."

"Yes."

"Does it help?"

"Well, I don't cut or think about killing myself all the time anymore."

"Shit. That's a start, right?" She hugs me again. "The other kids, they tease you?"

"Some do, behind my back. They stopped doing it to my face when I lost my temper and punched one of them and broke his stupid nose." I look into Mazie's eyes and smile a little at the memory. "I got suspended for three days. But my parents didn't punish me. GeeGeema said it was the best thing I could've done."

"I agree with her. Kids are bastards. Aren't there any other trans kids at your school?"

I sniff and shake my head. "I'm on meds, but I'm not trans. But school's awful. It's small and people aren't very accepting. Nobody who's different is out. After what's happened to me, I don't blame them for hiding until they leave. Some kids aren't allowed to sit near me in class or even talk to me. There's trouble with the bathrooms because, well, because. I have to use the one in the office but that's fine with me—it's private and doesn't stink. And I can't take PE, which I hate anyway, because of the locker rooms. But whatever happens there, I can put up with because I only have this year left and then it's over with. Right now, everyone just leaves me alone."

"You must be so lonely. No wonder you're heartbroken over Jimmy. I would be too. I feel even guiltier for taking him away from you."

"It wasn't your fault."

"I know. But still. Kaz. Please, look me in the eyes. It's always best to look up."

I lift my face.

"I don't care about any of that stuff." Mazie says, softly. "You're plain old you to me too. Do you understand?"

"You mean it?"

She smiles at me. "Of course I mean it—I never lie to friends! Look, I know people who are trans, and I know you said you weren't, but nobody I know is like you, so if I'm talking about you, are you a her and she? I mean, what do you prefer?"

"I use her and she. It's easier."

"You sure? Her and she?"

I nod.

"All right. Now, let's say I want to compliment you, do I say you're pretty, or handsome, or what?"

"I'm not pretty or handsome," I reply.

Mazie rolls her eyes; she looks like a kid. "Cripes, Kaz. Let's say, *theoretically*, that in some alternate universe I want to compliment you. Do you want me to say you're pretty and beautiful, or handsome and good-looking? Or are you letting me pick the gender?"

I smile. "'Alternate universe?' Pretty and good-looking."

"One from each. You going to be all right?"

"Yeah. I thought I was done crying."

"Nobody's ever done crying."

"I wish I would never cry again."

"Not a good wish. Listen, I'm sure there are people who would be happy to be your friends if you'd let them."

I shake my head. "I don't think so."

"Why not?"

"You mean besides the whole 'I'm not a girl' thing?" I count off on my fingers. "I'm dumb, I'm ugly, I'm boring, I'm too skinny, and I'm too tall."

Mazie stands, grabs my arms, and pulls me to my feet. "Now, you listen to me! You're not dumb, because you can carry on a conversation better than most adults. You're not ugly, at all. You're not boring because you just got half-naked in a cemetery. And as far as being too tall and too skinny goes..."

She stops talking.

"What?" I'm confused.

She's mad. "Stand up straight. I hate people who slouch! You look me right in the eyes. Are you taller than me?"

"No. We're the same."

She puts her hands on her hips, measuring their width, then mine. "Are your hips skinnier than mine?"

"No."

"Are we too tall and skinny?"

"I guess not." I don't know what she wants me to say.

"That wasn't an 'I guess not' kind of question! Yes or no. Are we too tall and skinny?"

"No. We're not too tall and skinny," I snap.

She steps back. "You're damned right we're not! Kaz, I like you, but if we're going to spend time together, you need to know that I don't like dumb people, I don't like ugly people, I don't like boring people, and I especially don't like people who are weak and scared. Understand?"

I nod.

"Kaz. *Do you understand?*"

"Yes, Mazie. I understand!"

It's a total surprise when she hugs me.

She takes a deep breath to calm herself down. "Look. It always makes me crazy when people I like put themselves down." She puts a hand where my neck meets my shoulder, squeezes a little, and smiles. "I'm sorry I let my temper show. Do you forgive me?"

An adult apologizing? "It's okay, Mazie. I get mad too."

"You sure?"

"Yeah. We're okay."

"One good thing." She pulls at my T-shirt—her T-shirt I'm wearing. "At least we got our clothes on straight."

I smile. "Yeah."

"Maybe next time we can go half-naked in the other direction and trade jeans—really give that old man with the beard something to look at!"

She smiles at me, and I blush. "I still don't think they'd fit."

"A boy-butt is a boy-butt, no matter who owns it." She winks, then she's serious. "You sure we're fine with each other?"

"Yes."

"Quite an afternoon we've had, us two. I'm glad you told me all those things, Kaz. It was brave of you, and friends shouldn't keep secrets from one another." She is so pretty when she smiles at me and crinkles her eyes like that!

She pulls out her phone and checks the time. "Yikes—I have to go! Can you meet me back here again, tomorrow, like around ten? Maybe we can talk more."

"Sure, Mazie. I'd like that."

"Thanks, Kaz." We give each other a hug. "You be extra-careful riding home."

I nod. "Okay. See you tomorrow."

*

MAZIE

I'll admit to a little surprise when Kaz-Fluff showed up. Wasn't sure she'd take the bait. When she appeared wearing a black tee, like I had on yesterday, I knew I was on the right track.

It was flat-out astonishment when she passed that little test of trading shirts. With her fear of being caught and disapproval, I considered her as far more risk averse. It didn't take much effort to make it happen. Normally, I would never part with any item as heavily loaded with my DNA as that tee. In this case, I'm playing, not adding to my list.

It was obvious when she finally decided to go along with the idea of trading. Once committed, she completed the act. I bet that's a regular pattern of behavior: Surprise, resistance broken with encouragement, acquiescence, and completion. Easy to exploit. She'd be an easy target for peer pressure. It's probably a good thing that she isolates.

Her recovery was quick with the brief lean against me. Wouldn't be surprised if it was planned, perhaps at a subconscious level, as a test of my reaction to physical contact. No objection from me. The more, the better!

I pretended to have missed her staring at me the second time I removed my shirt. Even if I hadn't caught her, I would've been able to tell, with a face so open. That blush she has is something else. It'll be a blast, eliciting that response on cue.

Chunky Dude's death leaves the perfect void for me to fill: Friend, confidant, a help against loneliness. I wondered at the deep attachment until the gender issues came to light. Then everything else became clear. More than support, it's acceptance she desires.

Not trans. Not a girl despite her appearance, but not male, nor nonbinary at this point. On meds, she said. With the unique physical build, I'd put money on dysphoria of some sort. Emotional sensitivity is a common side-effect of pubertal blockers—which helps explain her feelings sitting so close to the surface. Certainly, is unaffected by the sometimes common weight gain. Thank God the pronouns of choice are she and her. Far less trouble for me!

I hope whatever meds are in use haven't stunted the development of a sex drive. That would put a damper on my fun. I need to discover her age since that will limit what I can do. Legal trouble with a minor would hamper adding to my list.

Not on the spectrum as I had thought, but shy and insecure. No wonder with what she's been going through. Extra credit for bravery; telling those secrets must've been tough. Definitely lacking emotional support. I don't know what program she's in, but it's crap and her counselors are idiots. I need to find out when her next session is because, if told, even a crap counselor would recognize me as a possible threat.

Likewise, resorting to violence to end torment. Indication of a crap school run by idiot administrators. Bonus points for the broken nose. That's one way to solve peer issues. And I thought I had a lousy high school experience.

Still, my opportunities are enhanced by those flawed systems.

The strong response to my first hug reinforces her need for support. Those long, lean arms wrapped around me... then, to get similar, following reactions. Starved for friendship and affection. A serious case of skin hunger. Without a doubt.

I thought I was going to faint when I wiped those tears from that sweet face. My hands and arms tingled so badly. I was afraid they'd start to shake.

The drill-sergeant, up-and-at-'em routine achieved immediate results. Not used to being handled in such a fashion. Easy to establish myself as the alpha not-male. She did show her temper, though. I was half-expecting a swing at my nose. The immediate apology defused that situation while allowing me to maintain control.

When I compared our builds, putting my hands on her

hips. I could feel them through her jeans. Jutting and angular. I have to figure out a way to try on the rest of her clothing. I bet it'd fit.

When we hugged for the last time, I wrapped my arms about her ribs and pulled her tight. Head, shoulders, chest, belly, hips, legs, matching the whole length of my body. There was no move to resist. Good sign indicating positive results in future endeavors.

I think of the moment she turned to me, her shirt in hand: brown, unblemished, smooth. Long, lean, completely flat-chested. Thin enough that I could count ribs. Areolas, nipples, goose bumps. Slender shoulders and arms. Collarbones. Neck. So lovely.

One thing for sure, the only way I can tolerate spending enough time to have some fun is to eliminate her whiny, woe-is-me, sad-bitch-ass attitude. I can't stand that shit.

The question, put succinctly: can I play a manipulative mentor to a gender-questioning kid? A wicked Wendy to her innocent Peter Pan? Perhaps, more appropriately, a Captain Hook. It should be an interesting experience. Depending on her age, maybe we'll take a little trip into Neverland.

All we need is a Tinkerbell!

*

SK'DOO

Starting at Descher, I follow new Edge. It points right back to Pond. So maybe no more surprises from here. I'm far past Silas, where before I could barely reach his trunk. It's interesting to see him from this side. I know he's the same tree, but things are different when you look at them from another direction.

New Edge lets me go to the far side of Outside Road, past the triangle of ground where Damps and Rise meet. I've never looked up Rise and Hill or across Damps and Flats from here. Sexton's is so far away. I can't stop looking because it's been so very long since so many things were new-new.

I glide into the trees that surround this side of Pond. It's so quiet, with no Deads speaking. There are so many new plants. Some of these trees are bigger than Ottmar. No wonder the squirrels run to play here. I look up to see the branches of the big trees hiding the sky. The ground is covered with old brown leaves and broken sticks. Here and there, where light shines through from above, things other than lawn grow. Baby trees. Pretty bushes covered in groups of three shiny leaves.

Along the side of Pond is long grass. I know it's not machined very often. I look up the side of Hill and see Elba standing tall.

I see Kazabee talking to Mazie.

On the side of Pond, there's a part of an old tree half-in half-out of the water. On it are three things. Wait... I know... I know... Quicks call this "Turtle Pond," so these are turtles? Turtles!

I've never been close to turtles. How interesting they are. And what a strange shape, sitting in the sun. I like them. So calm and quiet. Different from squirrels, birds, chipmunks, and frogs, but a little like toads.

They don't seem to know I'm near. I look close at the one in the middle and press in against its tiny head...

I feel no zing but I'm not where I was. I'm down low, near the grass and water. I look to my side and there's a turtle looking right at me. I look to the other side. Another turtle. I'm turtle! I grow...afraid and pull away.

No zing and I'm not turtle, I'm me. I think. Maybe I'm not me, but I know I'm not turtle. I wonder, would being turtle be such a bad thing?

Leaving turtle, I glide out over the water to the Dead I know is there. I stay in the corner of new Edge. And wait.

I watch as Kazabee and Mazie hug. They leave. I stay.

"My name is Pat."

"Hello, Pat," I think, though I'm sure the Dead can't hear.

Chapter Five

KAZ

"Where you off to this morning?"

"No place, GeeGeema, I'm just going for a bike ride."

"A bike ride?"

"Yeah. It helps me think. I want to go before it gets too hot." I bend down and give her a quick squeeze. The memory of hugging Mazie flashes through my mind, and I give a little shiver.

"You okay, baby?"

"Yeah, GeeGeema. I had trouble sleeping last night."

I put Preston's half-a-green-can of stinky-chicken on

the floor, get a cup of water, place it in the middle of the table, and head for the door.

"You be careful on your bike ride."

"I will, GeeGeema. Bye-bye."

"And I love you too!"

*

Mazie's in her car when I arrive. She rolls down her window and squints into the sunshine. "Too hot out there today. How about we sit in the car?"

"I don't know..."

"You don't know what? If it's too hot in the sun?"

I grin. "No, you know..." I put my hands on my hips and use a deep, serious voice. "Never get in a stranger's vehicle."

"Oh, for God's sake!" She gets out of the car dressed all in black. When she steps away, its doors lock. She hands me her phone. "Here."

"What's this for?"

"It's the key, dummy. Watch." She walks over to the car and nothing happens. "Now, you come here."

As soon as I get near, the doors unlock.

"The car and phone talk to each other. Without the phone, the car won't run. Get it? So, if I start doing any weird-ass, stranger-danger shit, all you have to do is open the door and get out."

"What if you lose your phone?"

"What?"

"What happens if you lose your phone? How do you get in?"

"I enter a code on the door here," she says, pointing to a row of numbers. "Once inside, I have a hidden key I can use to start the car. Or I can push a button and talk to a person through the car, they verify who I am, and start it for me."

"Wow."

"So, are you fine with being in the car, or what?"

"Okay. Yeah."

"Good." She opens the driver's door and sits down. "Climb in the other side. I'm dying out here!"

It's dark inside. Seats and dash. The tint makes it even darker. The air starts cooling us when we close the doors. All automatic.

Mazie looks at me and smiles. "Like it?"

"Sure do. I love cars." It's true—I do.

Mazie's hands make tiny squeaks as she twists them on the steering wheel. "Me too. I always buy the ones I like. Never the top of the line because I hate leather seats. Too hot in the summer and too cold in the winter. Especially in shorts or minis. Cloth is better—never sticky. Always just right."

"I like the tint."

"It came tinted, but I ordered extra. I think it makes the car look a little more custom. You can barely see inside, but it's street legal. Don't want no hassle with the po-po."

"Po-po?"

She gives me a lopsided smile. "Po-po. The police? That's what we called them. Y'know, back in the day. Cripes, Kaz, way to make me feel ancient."

"Sorry."

"No problem." She smiles, eyes crinkling. "We're better off sticking to the present." She points to one of two water bottles in the console. "That one's yours."

"Thanks." I crack it open and take a sip.

A grin. "Aren't you afraid of me drugging the water?"

"I wouldn't drink it if it was unsealed."

"Really?"

"Really."

Mazie takes a drink from hers. "It doesn't bother you, being in this car? I mean, after what happened to Jimmy?"

"It is a little weird. Especially if I think about it too much."

She reaches over and puts her hand on my arm. Her fingers are so warm. "If it troubles you, we can go sit on the bench."

"No. I'll be okay. Let's stay here."

She spends several minutes showing me all the things the car can do. It's fancy. At the end, she turns the player up so loud that we have to shout to hear each other.

She shuts the music off. "I'll never understand the idiots who crank their systems so loud you can hear it a block away. Besides being bad for your hearing, it attracts the attention of the cops."

I grin, making sure to hide my gums. "You mean the po-po?"

"Hey!" A mock-stern look. "No making fun! I hardly ever use the sound system." She puts her hand on the wheel and slides them around, as if she's turning it. "I am here to drive, baby!"

She looks like a little kid. That makes me smile.

"It must cost a lot, this car."

"I like only the best things." She winks at me. "Like you."

I blush. "What do you do?"

"For work? I'm a C-Suite negotiator."

"What the heck is that?"

She laughs. "Let's see... First, it's 'C' like the letter." She draws the letter in the air with her left hand. "That stands for 'Chief.' That's the big bosses in a business: CEO, COO, CIO."

"Okay." The letters mean nothing to me.

"And then, 'Suite' because their offices are usually more than one room. So, C-Suite is slang for the most important people running a company."

"But what do you do?"

"I'm getting to that. In really big businesses, C-Suites make hundreds of millions of dollars a year and perks on top of that."

"Perks?"

"It's short for perquisites. It's things like extra vacation, bonus money, stock options, luxury cars, use of vacation homes, jets, yachts, chauffeurs... Don't forget separation pay—that can be hundreds of millions, all by itself."

"Wow."

"No fooling, 'wow.' When one of these people, mostly men by the way, moves from one company to another, they want to get the best deal because they're rich and powerful, and rich and powerful men always want to be richer and more powerful."

"That's what GeeGeema says."

"GeeGeema's right."

"And you do that? Get them the best deal?"

"No, but I wish. Then I'd own twenty-three of these cars! It's the lawyers who cut the deal. My job is to help the lawyers because sometimes everybody gets stubborn. When they do, I remind them that arguing isn't the only way to solve a problem."

"Is it hard to get them to listen?"

"When I need to remind them that I'm smarter than they are, I let them see me finish crosswords and write triple acrostic poetry, in ink, using French and German."

"Triple what?"

"Triple acrostic poetry. It's a kind of word puzzle."

Something to look up. "Your job sounds hard."

She shrugs. "It all comes down to reading people. I watch for changes in their faces, breathing, posture, heart rate, perspiration, changes in their voice. Little things tell you a lot about the other person. I also coach people we represent on how to appear more confident and less nervous than they might feel."

"Rich and powerful men get scared?"

Mazie laughs. "You bet. They might pretend they're not, but they can't fool me!"

"You went to school for that?"

"Not at all. I studied philosophy."

"What's that?"

"Philosophy? It's sort of hard to explain. Um... I suppose it's learning how to think, though a friend once called it 'organized bullshit,' and that's as good a definition as any. For sure there's a ton of bullshit to wade through with C-Suites, so maybe it was good training after all." She looks at me and smiles.

"You're so pretty." I put my hand over my mouth. "I'm sorry, I didn't mean to say that. It just sort of popped out!"

Her face softens. She blinks, slowly, then smiles and touches my hand. "Thank you, Kaz. That's always nice to hear."

We sit for a moment.

"Mazie, can I ask you a question?"

"You may always ask anything."

"When we first met, you said a friend of yours was here on the hill." I point out the window. "But all the graves up here are old."

She looks at me and frowns. "Kinda ruining our fun, Kaz."

"I'm sorry. You don't have to tell me if you don't want to."

Mazie pauses. "I must not've been clear. She was cremated. Her ashes were scattered down there"—she gestures—"in the pond."

"In the pond? Is there a gravestone for her?"

A headshake. "She didn't want one."

"Why not?"

"Don't know."

I can tell it was a mistake mentioning this, so I shut up. Mazie sighs. For a second, it seems like she might cry.

"I don't know if I should tell you this after what you told me yesterday. She hung herself. A belt around her neck. Leaned from a doorknob."

I reach over and touch her arm. "I'm sorry."

She looks at me, black eyes shining. "I suppose it's one way to make your problems go away."

I blink back tears. "Yeah." Then, I ask quietly, "You ever think about doing it?"

"Suicide?" She reaches over and puts the palm of her hand on the side of my face. She's so serious. "Life has taught me that I make my biggest mistakes when I fail to see what's really under my control. You can always change what you don't like. You remember that."

She takes her hand away. We sit a little while.

"So," she says. "Tell me about this 'not a girl' thing."

"I don't really want to talk about it."

"Hey. Friends. No secrets. Right? I didn't want to talk either."

Silence.

"Okay." I sigh. "I have a kind of gender dysphoria."

"I have no idea what that is."

I sort of grit my teeth. "I'm stuck because I can't decide if I want to be female or male or nonbinary and going through puberty scares me so bad that I can't deal."

"That's a thing?"

"It is for me."

"So?" Mazie says slowly.

I look out the window at old and tilting gravestones. "So, ever since I was little, I wasn't sure what I was. At first, I didn't even know it was a problem—I thought everyone was like me. Then I knew something was wrong, but I didn't know what it was. It got bad when my friends started going through puberty. The females grew boobs and butts and got their periods, and the males grew muscles and beards and their voices changed. That's when I started freaking because I didn't want *any* of that stuff happening to me. Then it turned out I was what GeeGeema called 'a late bloomer' which was fine by me."

"So..."

"So, I talked to Mom and Dad."

"That must've taken some guts."

"Tell me about it. When I started growing taller, I stopped eating because I hoped that would keep me from changing. Didn't work, of course."

"Of course."

"I started cutting because I didn't know how else to deal with it. I got caught doing that, and they took me to a therapist. At first, she thought I was dysmorphic. That's kinda when you don't like what your body looks like or what it's starting to look like, which sort of fit what I was going through. But once I told her about everything I was feeling, we figured out it was dysphoria. She helped me tell Mom and Dad. That was the really scary part." I tear up and wipe my eyes. Almost whispering, now. "I was afraid they'd stop loving me, or something."

"How did they take it?"

"Pretty good. Mom was confused and Dad was...Dad was sort of okay with it. They knew it was really messing me up, so we were referred to a gender specialist. We decided that maybe the best thing to do was to put me on meds to keep me where I was, so I had more time to decide."

I take Mazie's hand and press the fingers to the inside of my left arm. "There. Can you feel it?"

Mazie smiles, takes my hand, and presses it to the same place on *her* left arm. "Long-term birth control."

She understands! "Yeah—like that. It's my second one. I did shots, at first. One of the side effects is that it can make you overemotional." I roll my eyes. "I have that one. At least it doesn't make my face break out. I really watch what I eat so I don't gain weight and the doctor said I should get lots of exercise. That's one of the reasons I ride my bike so much."

"When did all this start?"

"The medicine? Three years ago. Since I turned fifteen."

"How long can you be on it?"

"I guess until I'm able to decide what to do. I see a counselor once every six weeks, but it doesn't seem to help." I frown. "It's group, which I don't like. My last session was a couple of days before Jimmy died. I was thinking about going back, but now I think I'll be able to do okay by myself."

"Do you still want to kill yourself?"

"Sometimes. But I won't because I know I would break GeeGeema's heart. The counselor says that someday I'll want to live because of me, but for now, it's okay to want to live for her."

"What happens now?"

"I'm supposed to decide if I want to be female, or start hormones and be male, or be nonbinary. Now that I'm on meds and everything has stopped, it's supposed to be easier because I'm supposed to feel a little more normal. Whatever that is."

"Yes." Mazie sort of laughs. "Whatever that is."

"Most kids take about a year to decide what they want to do, or what they can do, and go from there. But I'm *really* stuck. That's why I don't like going to group. I see other kids moving on and it upsets me. I'm also the oldest so I feel like I'm a bad example for the ones just starting." I shrug.

"What do the counselors tell you about being really stuck?"

"That I should be patient. Y'know. Everyone has their

own path and I shouldn't rush and blah-blah-blah. I know Mom and Dad want me to decide. I have college coming up, if I can pass calc, and I'd like to decide before then. Now, not deciding is almost as bad as not being able to decide!" I look at Mazie. "And that's all the weird stuff about me."

She touches my arm. "Thanks for telling me this, Kaz."

I twist in my seat and hug her as best I can. "Thanks for listening. It feels good to talk to somebody who doesn't take notes!"

"I can't imagine not being a girl."

"In counseling, I learned that being a girl's different from being female."

"Fine." Mazie snaps. "I can't imagine not wanting to be a girl *or* female." She looks at me. "Were you a tomboy?"

"The counselors don't like that word."

She glares, eyes narrow. "I don't see any goddam counselors in the car, do you? It's a simple question. Were you a tomboy?"

She's mad, like yesterday. I remind myself to not correct her.

"Yeah, I was, completely. Didn't like any girl stuff. I was always climbing trees and playing in the dirt. Learned to spit. Played war. Loved to wrestle and tickle. Back then, I didn't understand why my parents made me stop doing that. Played with trucks and cars. I still really like cars. Always wanted boy's clothes. I don't think I ever played dolls or dress-up. Ever." I smile. "My jammies and sheets had cowboys on them."

"But you don't want to be a boy?"

I think *or male,* but I don't say that. "Maybe I want to be one but not look like one. That's part of what I can't figure out. The thought of changing into a male scares me even more than having boobs, a big butt, and a period. I mean, an Adam's apple would be bad enough. I have no idea what I'd do if I grew a..." I glance at my crotch. "—you know." I blush.

Mazie smiles at me. "A 'you know' has its uses, you know. I was a part-time tomboy."

"Part-time?"

"My parents were divorced. I lived with my mom during the school year and my dad in the summer. Mom was all about dressing up and playing nice. As soon as vacation started, I was with Dad. The first thing he'd do is take me to his barber, and I'd get a short, boy's haircut. I'd grow it out for the rest of the summer. With him, it was T-shirts, jeans, and mostly bare feet." She looks and me and grins. "You look like a tree climber."

I laugh. "All the time. Up on the roof too. Mom was always yelling that I'd fall and break my neck."

"She was right." Mazie smiles, lifts her chin, and points to a faint scar. "From falling out of a tree. And I did almost break my damned neck."

"Ouch." I show her a long, pale line on the underside of my left arm. "Jumping from a swing. Got caught on the chain. You never saw so much blood!"

"Sounds like we're two of a kind." She laughs. "I remember, when I was real little, in the summer, all I wore was cutoffs. Dad always said he 'didn't have time for any girly shit.'"

I laugh with her. "Is he still like that?"

She looks down, then out at woods past the pond. "He died when I was twenty-three. Heart attack. Mom was killed in a car accident a couple years later."

"Oh, Mazie. I'm sorry." Twenty-three's only five years older than me!

More silence.

"What do your parents do?"

"Mom's a programmer. Dad does database stuff."

"You get along with them?"

"I suppose. They're my parents. Y'know?"

"I sure do know. Brothers or sisters?"

"Nope." I shake my head. "Just me. How about you?"

"Dad was in the insurance business. Mom worked in a store. They had a son. He died when I was a junior in college."

"You miss him?"

Mazie sighs and looks out the side window. "We never

got along. Being with him was always very difficult and I've found that life is better without him." She looks at me and shrugs.

I lay my hand on hers. "That's too bad."

"That's the way the world is." She smiles a little.

"Your bracelet is very pretty," I say, hoping to lift the mood.

"You like?" She moves her right wrist to make it sparkle. "Here." She works the clasp and removes it. "You try."

I feel little zings when she holds my left arm and wraps the jewelry around it.

"Oh, Kaz, look how nice it is against your skin."

"It's so heavy! Is it real gold?"

"Sweet-Kaz," she laughs. "I wear only real gold. It's eighteen carat. I like a more masculine style, so that's a man's bracelet. As nice and slender as your arms are, I think you'd look much better wearing a woman's version. It's called a Greek box chain. Very strong. A little uncommon too."

I look closely, studying the links and trying to figure out how they hold on to each other. Another thing to look up. "Greek box chain. It's beautiful. How long have you had it?"

A big smile. "I bought it with the first check from my C-Suite work. I hardly ever take it off, and when I do, it never leaves my sight. Of all the things I have, I love it best."

I try to work the clasp but can't.

"Let me." She takes my arm and turns it over, palm up. Sliding her hand along my scar, she takes the clasp in the fingers of one hand, gives a little twist, and it pops open. "See? Easy." She holds out her right arm, same way, palm up. "Now. You put it on me."

I fumble a little but manage to get it hooked. When I look up at her, she has a funny smile on her face.

She looks at my right hand. "What are those scars from?"

"These?" I show them to her.

She takes my hand and gently rubs the scratch marks with her thumb. She looks in my eyes and speaks quietly. "Are they from you? Cutting? Or, I hope, another tomboy adventure?"

"GeeGeema's cat, Preston, gave me those. He doesn't like being petted by anybody but her."

"I don't think I like Preston very much." She kisses the scars, then lets me go. "There. All better." She grins.

It happens so quick, I don't have time to blush.

"Tell me about GeeGeema."

"She's my mom's mom's mom."

"Must be old."

"Ninety-seven."

"That's old. She do all right?"

I shrug. "She's ninety-seven. She gets around. Has a little trouble hearing, but not too bad. Has macular degeneration, that's probably the worst thing."

"How bad is it?"

"She only sees clearly in one spot in one eye. It can't be fixed. I suppose someday she'll be blind. If she lives that long."

"Is she sick?"

"No. Not at all, but she says the line between being here and *not* being here is pretty thin to start, and when you're as old as she is, it gets so there's hardly any line at all."

Mazie smiles. "Sounds pretty smart."

I smile back. "She is. When she first moved in, I thought she was sort of dumb and confused. But it's all an act. She's the smartest person I know."

"I never had any grandparents. You're lucky to have her."

"I know. I worry, you know, about her dying."

"You ever tell her that?"

"Once. She laughed and said anybody can die, anytime, and that she'd miss me, if I died first." I smile.

"You're so pretty too, Kaz."

I blink. Then blush.

"There's nothing I'd love more than to spend the afternoon getting to know all about you, but"—Mazie points at the car's clock—"I need to scoot. Is that all right?"

"Yeah. Sure."

"Can you give me my phone?"

"Phone?"

"Yes. My phone. It's the car key, remember?"

"Oh, yeah. Duh." I hand it to her.

She places it on the seat between her legs. "Would it okay be if I texted you?"

"Sure. Except I don't have a phone."

"No phone?"

"It got wet. I'm getting a replacement next month."

"No problem." She leans across, pops open the dash compartment, and points to a phone inside.

"I can't take a phone from you!"

She waves her hand. "Sure, you can. Use it until you get your own, whenever that is, then give it back. It's a prepaid. I always have a couple."

"Why?"

A shrug. "I break a lot of phones."

Mazie gives me the code to unlock it and helps me set up an account in a messaging system she uses. "It's not super-fast, and it won't work as a hot spot. Don't connect to any networks. It has a ton of hours, use them instead. It won't ring, but it'll buzz on its softest setting. You can use it for email and Internet and stuff like that, but I text only in the app we just used to set up your account. It won't save anything 'cause my business is my business."

We get out of the car.

"Don't bother giving the number out because I'll toss it once the hours are gone. And don't go telling anybody that you have it either. I don't want to have to start handing out phones to all your jealous friends."

"I don't really have any friends."

Mazie walks over to me, bumps my shoulder with hers, and smiles. "Sure, you do, Kaz. You have me!"

Smiling, I bump her back. "Thanks."

"One more rule about the phone." She's serious now. "*Never* use it when you're with me. I mean no talking, no texting, no looking, no ringing, no buzzing, no nothing. I promise to give you my undivided attention when we're to-gether. I expect exactly the same amount of respect from you. Do you understand?"

I nod. "I understand. I mostly use a phone to let Mom and Dad know where I'm at, but since they don't know I have this one, I won't be doing that. The only person I ever texted was Jimmy, so..." I shrug. "Not using it won't be a problem. I promise to turn it off when I'm with you."

"That's my Kaz." She smiles, holds out her arms, and beckons with her hands. "Now, let's give each other a big hug. Then, I suppose, I'll have to let you get you home to

GeeGeema."

Nobody really hugs me hard anymore. Mazie's so warm. It's good to be held. I feel like I could go on forever but we both let go before it starts getting weird.

Mazie gets back in her car. "Are you sure you have a charger that'll fit?"

I check the port. "Yeah. It's like my old one."

"And you're sure it's all right if I text you tonight?"

I smile. "Sure, I'm sure."

"Thanks, Friend-Kaz. Be good!" She drives away.

I tuck the phone in my rear pocket, make sure it won't fall out, get on my bike, and head home.

*

MAZIE

Getting her into the car wasn't difficult. Being in a controlled environment makes everything so much easier. She's still cautious though, not drinking from unsealed bottles of water. A good idea, considering the times we live in.

Genuine interest in the vehicle gives us something else in common, besides the death of Chunky Dude. I can use that to draw us closer together. Her showing her sense of humor and joking with me is an excellent sign. A test of my tolerance for being teased. The back-and-forth helps establish us as equals in her mind.

She seemed interested in what I do, though I'm not sure how much of it she understood except that I'm well paid. Curiosity can be good, especially when it's steered. Allows one thing to lead to another.

Philosophy. Sure. Philosophy 101. What a joke that crap was, but I couldn't tell her what I really studied.

Her recall and challenge of my statement about my friend on the hill was the real surprise. I hadn't expected to be asked to explain. I did a reasonable job of turning it into a sad loss in my life, something else to increase our bond. But me not anticipating her questions—that's a sign that I underestimated her. I'll not let it happen again.

Turning that conversation into a lever compelling her to talk about her dysphoria was a nice touch. Cutting, considering suicide. She is so confused with herself. I need to drive that home as often as I can.

Her correcting me though, can't have that. I'll apply outbursts of temper until it stops. Shouldn't take long to modify that behavior since she works to avoid conflict whenever possible.

No siblings. That's good. I need to be careful of Gee-Geema. An obviously powerful influence. I'll make establishing a wall of secrecy a higher priority.

Getting her onto one of my phones, something I

thought would be a struggle, was one of the easiest things I've ever managed. Pure, dumb luck that she's without a phone. I hope everything else goes as smoothly.

Besides a few light touches, which we both enjoyed, and one good hug, there was disappointingly little physical contact. If I want to have any fun at all, I need to take steps to change that as soon as possible. And I can do that without fear of legal entanglements. Now I know she's of age and there will be no meddling counselors, I'll start pushing harder, starting tonight.

One thing I'll say about her—she has great taste in jewelry!

*

Bzz...

M: KZ?

K: Hi!

M: Are you awake? Dumb question, I know. Duh.

K: Yes. I'm awake.

M: Doing what?

K: Trying to sleep.

M: Same here. You in bed? Cowboy
jammies?

> *K:* Too hot for jammies. Just a tee.
> Um... Your tee.

M: Mine? From yesterday? How
nice!

And cowboy undies?

> *K:* Your tee and my undies, but no
> cowboys :)

M: I bet you look cute. Hot there?
No air?

> *K:* We have air but it's not set cold to
> save $.

M: Gotcha. It's cool here. I need a
blanket.

> *K:* I wish.

M: But still no jammies. No tee. No nothing.
  Try it!

You sleepy?

> *K:* Not really.

M: Me, either.

K: Been thinking.

M: Bout what?

K: Today. Thanks for listening.

M: Thanks for talking. You taught
me a lot.

Sorry for getting a little mad.

K: S'OK. Don't worry about it.

M: Hug was nice.

K: Yes. Hug was nice.

M: I'm thinking about you wearing
my tee.

Us trading, yesterday. That was fun.
Yes?

K: Yes. But scary. People could see.

M: There were no people to see. Just
us. We're brave. Right?

K: I guess.

M: Like now. Just us, with no people
to see.

We're brave. Right?

K: I guess.

M: KZ... We're brave... Right?

K: Right.

M: Good.

K: Can I ask a question?

M: You may always ask anything.

K: Your tan. It has no lines?

M: Ha. You noticed when we traded tees?

Observant and smart.

You're right. No lines. Wait...

<image naked back MZ>

K: How do you do that?

M: What? No lines? How do you think?

K: Tanning bed?

M: Nope. Outside in the sun. No top.

K: Where?

M: Backyard. There's a high fence.

Wait...

M: See? No lines, anyplace.

Outside in the sun. No bottom.

There's a *very* high fence.

K: I could never do that.

M: Sure, you could. You're brave. Like me.
It's easy!

But no sunburns... Ouch!

K: Your muscles look nice. You're so
pretty.

M: Thanks. Your turn!

K: ???

M: Do you have tan lines?

K: No. No tan lines.

M: No pictures. No proof.

K: I can't do that!

M: Just us, with no people to see. We're
brave. Right?

KZ? You still there?

KZ?

>*K:* You can't show *anybody* else.
>
>You promise?
>
>I mean it. I would be so mad!
>
>You promise?

M: I would never share! Just don't
show your face. It's easy!

NO SHARING. I promise!

>*K:* OK. Wait...
>
>*<image naked back KZ>*

M: KZ you're pretty. Now the other,
please.

KZ...

Now the other. Please?

>*K:* Wait...
>
>*<image naked backside KZ>*

M: KZ your boy-butt is *very* pretty.

And it's true. No tan lines!

>*K:* Cause I have no tan!

M: Laughing. Funny.

Thanks for the pictures. You are very
brave.

Your skin is beautiful. Very pretty.

I love those little dimples in your
lower back.

Now you're without tee and undies.

You're naked! And cooler, like me!

>*K:* Yes. No tee and undies. Naked.

M: It's fun being naked with you!

>*K:* MZ...

>PLEASE don't share those pictures.

>I don't like them. I am too skinny.
>No muscles.

>I'm not pretty.

M: I promise. No sharing. Just us.
No sharing mine, either!

You are slender, NOT skinny. Muscles are not needed.

Perfect. Pretty.

>*K:* OK... If you say so.

Can I ask another question?

M: You may always ask anything.

K: Why are you so nice to me? I'm
not special.

M: !!! You are special. Special to me.

K: You are beautiful. I am not.

M: Stop saying that! You ARE good-
looking.

K: Don't think so.

M: Your pictures show you're pretty.

Your back and boy-butt are very
pretty.

K: Maybe.

M: I looked when you had your shirt
off...

Your front is pretty, too.

K: You looked?!

M: You looked at me. No tan lines.
Remember?

K: Oh. Yeah.

M: Don't blush (ha)! It's OK to look
at me. I don't mind.

Happy to show you anything you
wish to see.

I bet you are pretty all over.

                 K: Not pretty like you.

M: Grrr... STOP IT!!!

                 K: Sorry.

M: S'OK. Now, let me ask *you* a
question...

Do all pretty people look like me?

                 K: No.

M: So... You can be pretty but not
look like me?

                 K: I guess.

M: You guess right, Pretty-KZ.

Tomorrow. Do you work?

                 K: Late afternoon. You?

M: Same. Want to meet at the pond?

                 K: Sure! When?

M: Is 10 too early?

> *K:* No. It's good.

M: You sure?

> *K:* It's perfect!

M: Like you!

> *K:* I'll be there!

M: Smiling. Time for sleep? Yes?

> *K:* Yes.

M: Wait...

<image puckered lips MZ>

M: A kiss goodnight.

> *K:* Wait...

> <image puckered lips KZ>

> *K:* That's a kiss back!

M: So nice. Maybe kiss for real next
time?

> *K:* Couldn't do that!

M: Just us, with no people to see.
We're brave. Right?

Sleep well, Naked-Brave-Pretty-KZ.

Try sleeping that way. It's cooler!

> *K:* I'll try. Night.

*

SK'DOO

"I kiss someone other than my spouse."

  "My coleslaw is the best."

  "Matthew Perry? The lousiest sailor I ever knew."

I like night. Everything's quiet. No Quicks. Well hardly any Quicks. Sometimes they sneak in. Then, I have fun by tripping them, or tingling their fingers, or touching their ears. I know it doesn't take much to scare Quicks in the dark.

  "Betty said mine was the biggest and Betty never lies."

Night used to be the best time to get around without Quick-made lightning, but that's not true anymore. They decorate Deads with lights that never die. I don't know how they work, but they make lightning during the day and use lightning at night, and it doesn't matter the direction, lightning is lightning. I'm kept away from whole sections of Dead. Who knows what they could be saying?

I stop at Dead Jimmy.

"I can catch that ball."

"I don't need to get a hundred on every test."

"Yeah, she's pretty, but her boobs could be bigger."

Then, I move to Pond, new Edge, and Dead Pat. I'm comfortable now, out on the water.

It doesn't take long. One after the other:

"I'm the fastest on my bike."

"Tomatoes—yuck!"

"My life is taken."

"They're real gold?"

Wait...wait... I stop and think... With all the things that all the Deads have told me, I hear those words, "my life is taken," only from Deads who have been made that way by others. Not by accident, and not in war, but on purpose.

I know Deads who become that way because of a Quick always say it. Always. Always. Even babies who have nothing else to say. All of them say those same words.

That means a Quick made Pat a Dead.

"My life is taken."

A repeat. I hear it, once more. No mistake.

Deads don't lie.

Chapter Six

KAZ

I must've looked at those pictures of Mazie's back and butt a million times before finally going to sleep. My pictures too.

I frown. It was dumb of me to send those images. I better not see them all over the Internet in a couple of days, or I will punch her in the nose. And that's for sure!

I went back into the app and our thread was gone. I checked the phone as closely as I could, and just like Mazie said, they weren't saved anywhere. At least anywhere I could find, and I'm pretty good at that kind of stuff.

She did say her business was her business. The prepaid

phones and the messaging she uses must help her keep it that way.

*

I'M SITTING ON the bench, pond-watching, when Mazie cruises up, her hair in a ponytail.

"Hey, good-looking! How long you been here?"

"Just a couple minutes." More like a half-hour.

"No need to be early with me, Kaz. I'm always right on time! And there will be no sitting around today. Lock your bike to something. We're going for a drive."

"In your car?"

That earns me an eye roll. "No, in the dirigible I have in my back pocket! Of course, in my car."

"Where we going?"

"No place. We'll just drive south a little, turn around, and drive back. An hour, or so."

"I don't know..."

"You don't know what? What am I? An axe-murderer? I thought we already settled that. You can hold my phone if you want. Kaz. Lock your bike to something. Come on. Let's go!"

"There's a rack down near the road."

"Whatever. You go first. I'll follow."

I coast down the hill. There, by the maintenance

building, is the rack. I lock my bike and climb in the car.

"Nice motor on your bike!" That's the first thing Mazie says.

"What?"

"I said you have a nice motor on your bike."

"My bike doesn't have a motor."

She looks at me, shakes her head a little, and smiles. "Never mind." As soon as the car moves forward the doors click to lock. "You want the phone?"

"No. I trust you."

"Good." Then a wide smile. "Ever ridden in an electric?"

"I've read all about them, but no. It's so quiet."

"That's what I like about them. You sail along. And this..."

We turn right onto the main road. She presses the gas pedal. I'm pushed back into my seat. Gasping, I look at the speedometer. Over a hundred miles an hour! She smiles, takes her foot off the pedal, and we slow down to a regular speed.

"That's scary!"

"Ever go that fast in a car before? Isn't it great?"

"Our cars would blow up if you tried to do that!"

Mazie laughs. "And there's this, that I told you about yesterday." She presses a button on the steering wheel, puts her hands in her lap, pulls her feet away from the pedals, looks at me, and grins. "Automatic pilot."

I look at the road. There's a sharp bend coming up. The car steers its way around it, adjusting its wheel and speed as it goes. "That's kind of scary too."

"It'll stop and go all by itself. Knows the speed limit. If I punch an address into the nav, it can sometimes take me all the way there with me just sitting here. It does take some getting used to."

"Yeah. I'd be way more relaxed if you steered."

"I understand, Kaz. I didn't trust it at first either." She pushes a button and takes over.

"Where are we going?"

"Like I said, no place. Just for a drive. It's nicer in here. Air-conditioned. Quiet. Private. No bugs."

"Uh...may I ask you a question?"

"You may always ask me anything."

"Are you glad you're female?"

"Big question, right there!" She scratches the back of her neck and looks at me, teasing. "You mean 'female pre-senting,' don't you?" Then she laughs. "Don't you talk about this stuff with your counselor?"

"Yeah. But they encourage us to ask people we trust. It's okay if you don't want to answer."

"You ask your mom this question?"

"If I did, we'd probably both die of blushing!"

Mazie laughs again. Glancing at me, she thinks for a second, then gets what GeeGeema would call "an ornery look."

"All right. Take off your tee."

"What?"

"I said, take off your tee."

"Why?"

"You want me to talk about maybe being glad to be female? Then take off your tee!"

"But…"

"I've already seen you without your shirt, remember? Hell, I've seen your boy-butt. Why don't you want to take off your shirt?"

"Besides that I'm embarrassed? Somebody else might see."

She nods at the windshield. "This blue car coming the other way. Look at the driver as hard as you can as it passes."

We zoom by in opposite directions.

Mazie glances at me. "What color shirt did he have on?"

"Couldn't tell. He went by too fast."

"Are you even sure it was a guy driving the car?"

"Um…no."

"We're in this car and we see each other, right? But people driving past. They don't see us, any more than we see them."

"Yeah. So?"

"Kaz, dear, to me, that's what being female, nonbinary, or male is. There's the part inside. Like where we're sitting, and the part outside, what others see when they drive past. One has hardly anything to do with the other. So, take off your tee."

"You mean that?"

"Hell yeah! I want to see you without your shirt! And don't use people seeing as an excuse because now you know that's not true. And don't use being embarrassed as an excuse either. I already saw you without a shirt when we traded. It's just us. Be brave, right?"

I hesitate, then lean forward and pull my T-shirt over my head. I cover the front of me with it as I drop my elbows. I have goose bumps all over.

Mazie's smiling at me. "You're so pretty." She reaches over and pulls my arms down. "Don't cover up! Let me see what you have!"

"Not much."

"Wrong. You're good-looking. Sit up straight in the seat! Wait...do you shave your armpits?"

I fold my arms tight against my sides. "Yeah, the meds don't stop that kind of hair. I tried growing it out, but I didn't like the way it looked. Is that girly? Shaving?"

"No. Some people shave all their hair off. Some don't

shave any." She looks at me and grins. "Now, for more talk about whether I'm glad I'm a female." She pushes a button and all the windows go down.

"What are you doing?" I lift my tee back up and cross my arms over my chest.

"Why are you covering up?" Her voice is loud over the wind noise.

"Because somebody might see!"

She laughs. "Somebody might see what? Your boobs? That's what you're covering, right?" She reaches over and pulls my arms down. "Look at yourself! You don't have any boobs. None! If somebody sees you, they're not gonna think 'look at that female's boobs,' they're gonna think 'that brown male with no armpit hair sure is skinny', especially if you sit up straight and put your shoulders back."

"Not if they know who I am."

She sighs. "Kaz, that's what I'm trying to tell you. Out here, nobody knows who you are. You can be anybody you want."

"You make it sound so easy."

"It is and it's not. It gets easier as you go."

"But are you glad you're a female?"

"I'm almost always underestimated because I'm female. And because I'm pretty, I can get away with causing trouble. I take advantage of those two things. Especially in my job."

"That doesn't seem fair."

"I'm sure you see the cute girls at school do it all the time. And the good-looking jocks getting away with all kinds of shit that the ugly, nerdy boys could never do." She shrugs. "It's the way the world is. I'm tougher and far smarter than most of the nonbinaries or males I know. But that doesn't have anything to do with being female. I'd be that way no matter what I was—or chose to be. Understand?"

"Maybe, a little."

"Have you forgotten you're not wearing a shirt?"

"Yeah, I did."

"To me, that's what being female is like. I pay attention to it, sometimes, but most of the time, I don't. If I went around all day thinking 'I'm female, I'm female, I'm female' I'd be even crazier than I am. Besides, I don't think being nonbinary or male makes much of a difference."

"What do you mean?"

"I know plenty of them who would never sit in a car, like you are right now, with the windows down and their shirts off."

"Why not?"

"Could be lots of reasons. They're shy, or they think they're skinny, or fat, or out of shape, or too hairy, or not hairy enough. Or their chest is too big, or not big enough. Who knows? Maybe their nipples are easily wind-burned!

Does your dad walk around the yard with his shirt off?"

"No."

"Could he?"

"Yes."

"See?"

*

SK'DOO

I move through the new woods, looking and listening, thinking about Dead Pat being buried in Pond.

Long ago, Deads were wrapped in cloth and placed in the ground. Then, they started putting Deads in wooden boxes. Now, they are in boxes that are inside boxes. But how is Dead Pat? In a boxed box? A box? Wrapped in cloth? I wonder.

The turtles are out at Pond. I now know that turtles are only on the sunken tree when the sun shines. Choosing the biggest, I zing in again. I don't try to do anything. I stay still.

When I was bird or chipmunk, everything happened quickly. Turtle is slow. It doesn't think it's slow but that everything else is fast. When it thinks, that is. Turtle isn't big on thinking.

It turns out that turtle is very stubborn, maybe because it doesn't think. After losing a slow argument, I decide the best thing to do, if I want to do anything, is suggest what I want and let turtle do the rest.

I-turtle sits on the log and lets the sun shine on us. I feel...warm. Being here is like Haven, except part of me is always paying attention, listening for trouble, and ready to move. I think about trying to turtle out into Pond, then decide I've been turtle for long enough. It's nice for sitting on a log, but it's not for me.

*

KAZ

Mazie switches on the automatic pilot.

"Now what are you doing?"

"Talking about whether I'm glad I'm a female."

Just like I did, she leans forward and takes off her black tee. Today, there's no bra. Nothing but her bracelet and no-line tan. She sits back, puts her arms on the rests with the seat belt between her breasts. She looks down at herself, then over at me. "So, now, if somebody sees me, what'll they think?"

"Look at those pretty boobs?"

"Ha! Probably more like *why isn't she wearing a shirt*?" She looks at me and smiles, her eyes twinkling.

I feel like I am flying.

"May I touch them?"

"My boobs? Sure. Touch away."

They're small with nipples standing out. I pet the side of the one closest to me. So soft. "They're very pretty."

"My boobs thank you."

I put my finger on Mazie's side and trace the muscles there. "I think your muscles are pretty too." I give her goose bumps.

She closes her eyes and tilts her head back against the seat. "Kaz. I'm ticklish. Good thing we have autopilot!"

"You work out?"

"I used to swim but thought it was making my shoulders too broad, so I gave it up. I like to run. I lift, a little. Not enough to bulk up—I like a smooth look. Martial arts too."

"Martial arts?"

"Being able to protect yourself is a good idea, female, nonbinary, or male."

I touch her breasts again, cupping one in my hand. Soft and hard, together. I feel like... I don't know what I feel like.

"I read they hurt, sometimes when you get your period."

Mazie nods. "That can happen."

"What's that like, having a period?"

She looks at me, surprised. "You don't menstruate?"

"No. I started my meds before that happened."

"Well, everyone's different."

"Is it messy? Does it hurt?"

"There are tampons and pads. I know a few women who have to go to bed with cramps. But like I said, everybody's different. If you started yours, who knows?"

"That's scary."

She shrugs. "They have hormones and stuff that help. Don't you look these things up on the Internet?"

"I do. But I like talking and asking questions. And the Internet's filled with liars and creeps. You never know who you're really talking to. Might be some old pervy guy!" I touch the underside of her breasts and pet them. We go over a bump in the road and they jiggle. I suddenly think of Preston running for his food. "And your boobs hurt when your period happens?"

"Some people's do."

"Do you like that they're small?"

"More comfortable. They don't get in the way. Better for running and exercise. It's easier to buy clothes and pretty bras. And I think smaller ones look better for longer."

"I thought guys liked bigger ones best."

"Not just guys, but people who only like big boobs are idiots."

"I'm afraid mine would be big."

"If I had big ones and didn't like them, I'd have them reduced." Mazie grins at me. "You can always change what you don't like."

"What feels best with them?"

"Anything that makes yours feel good."

She takes control of the car and pulls over into an empty parking lot where an old gas station used to be. "And here we are!"

I panic a little. "What are you doing?"

"Relax, Kaz." She puts a hand on my tummy. It's her first touch and it ripples through me. "This is where we turn around."

She shifts the car into park and puts the windows up, unlocks her seatbelt, then mine. She turns to me and runs her hands over my skin. It feels so good that my brain almost shuts off.

"And this is where we switch places so you can drive back."

"Drive? I can't drive your car!"

"Sure, you can. I'm fully insured. But it's not free."

"Not free?"

"Nothing ever is. The price you pay is us switching places half-dressed as we are."

"Somebody might see!"

"Why are you always so worried about what people might see?" She tilts her head toward the highway. "People are in their own cars, speeding by, remember? They don't care what we do as long as we're not in their way."

Mazie is crazy. *Crazy Mazie*, I think. I grab the door handle. "Okay...now?"

She laughs. "No! There are rules." She runs two fingers along my collarbone, rests them in the hollow of my throat for a second, then rubs the top of my chest. "When you get out, you have to stand up, straight. We go around the back of the car. We take our time. No running. You break the rules and we start over."

I nod distractedly. "Yeah. Like a game." When I step out of the car, I feel completely naked. I close my eyes...remember...skinny brown male. With no armpit hair. I stand up straight and put my shoulders back. I want to run but when I look over at Mazie, she's acting as if being outside without a shirt is the most natural thing in the world.

We walk to the back of the car. Just as we meet, she steps in front of me, wraps her arms around me, and gives me a hug so strong that my back pops. I feel her boobs smoosh up against me. She's always so warm! She looks at me, smiles, and kisses me right on the lips, not sloppy, but like a kiss from those old movies that GeeGeema and I watch.

She lets go and starts walking, giving me a hard smack on my boy-butt as we pass. I kind of like that.

We're both laughing when we slam and lock the doors.

"There. That was a perfect bit of fun, wasn't it?"

I look at her and bite my lip.

"Kaz…do you not want me to kiss you?"

"Yes. I mean no. I mean you kissing me is fine."

"Have you been kissed before?"

"Just family and like that." I lower my eyes. "I've never done any of this stuff before."

"Oh, I'm sorry, sweetheart. Being kissed, and all the rest of this so soon."

"No, it's okay. I'm glad you were my first kiss." I look and smile at her. "It was perfect." She's so pretty. I reach and touch her lips. "This is all perfect."

She leans over, kisses me again, and pulls back.

"And there's your second one."

She takes the band from her ponytail and her black hair falls to frame her beautiful face. She kisses me again, this time grabbing the hair on the back of my head and pulling me close. My eyes roll as I kiss her harder and put my hands on her ribcage, running them up to her breasts. Her skin is warm and smooth and I feel her muscles beneath. As she pulls away, she touches my lips with the end of her tongue, giving me the shivers. When I breathe out, it's shaky.

"And that's your third." She opens her eyes and lets go of my hair.

My hands are still on her skin. "Do I kiss okay?"

She looks at me like I'm a paper she's grading. "Accepta-ble, for a beginner. Likely to improve with practice."

"You're funny."

"I'm serious." With a soft, dreamy look on her face, she pushes my hands away and puts her right hand against my chest with her first two fingers and thumb spread right above my collarbones. She pushes me back into my seat and holds me there for a few seconds. Her eyes are closed. I can see her breathing. I feel dizzy from her touch and sit up straighter because she doesn't like it when I slouch. She takes a deep breath and holds it as she slides her hand down across my chest to my belly button.

It feels so good that I take a deep breath. She turns her hand and moves it so her little finger skims along, just inside the top of my jeans.

I pull my tummy in to give her more room, but I don't know if I want her to stop or keep going. It's confusing. It feels almost like being stuck.

Mazie opens her eyes, looks right into mine, like she's in a trance, then she exhales and takes her hand back, rub-bing her fingers against her thumb.

"Are you a lesbian?"

She smiles, leaning in to rub noses. "What makes you ask that, Kissy-Kaz?"

"I don't know? Like, maybe us? Right now?"

She turns her head slightly, looking at me through narrowed eyes. "*Never* turn a statement into a question unless your goal is to be perceived as weak and immature." Then, sitting back. "As far as my orientation's concerned... I don't like idiots—any idiots. And lots of men are idiots. Lots of everyone are idiots. I'll tell the truth because we're friends and friends don't lie. It's not like I've had hundreds of partners, but I like nice, I like easy on the eyes, and I like nonidiots. Other things don't matter so much. Do you understand?"

"Yes. I understand."

"Besides, you're not sure if you're female, male, boy, girl, cis, straight, queer, binary, nonbinary, fluid, non, or whatever other permutation there might be, so even if you were the only person I ever kissed, we still wouldn't know about me *or* you." She smiles a little and runs her fingers along the side of my neck. "Would we?"

"I guess not."

I get one more kiss. "The answer is yes, I'm glad I'm a female *and* I'm glad I'm a woman. Now, let's put our shirts on the right way round and have you carefully drive us back."

*

MAZIE

Now, *that's* more like it! In the car without too much fuss. Next time there will be no hesitation.

Making up answers to a few silly questions was a small price to pay for all that skin. Lovely, lovely, lovely skin on such a lovely, lovely, lovely body. Perfect.

As predicted, her token resistance to taking the next step is easily broken with the smallest push. Her willingness to comply signals great opportunity. Continual changes to the situation keep her off balance. She is unable to regain control but adapts well.

I knew Kaz lacked sexual experience but didn't realize to what extent. To know that she's never been touched makes it more exciting. And to be the first person she's ever touched with those long, thin, cool fingers. It's...delightful.

Kissing her virgin mouth. Putting my hand on her throat. Sensing the flow of air. Feeling her skittering pulse, almost twice a normal rate. Pressing hard enough to start restricting the flow of blood was delicious. One step removed from heaven. It was fortuitous that she adjusted her posture. It helped me break my concentration and enabled me to continue.

I was so tempted to run my hand down the front of her jeans. I knew she was willing, or could have been made willing to my advances, but I'm glad I resisted. Saving those last few inches of flesh for another day makes it all the more interesting for me.

And I need to stop using that old "motor on the bike" joke. Nobody ever gets it!

*

Bzz...

M: Did we have fun today?

K: YES! YES! YES!

M: What did you like best?

K: All of it!

M: List in order.

K: I can't.

M: You can. List.

K: OK...

Kissing.

Talking and Touching (tie).

No shirts.

Driving.

M: Wait... Driving is last?

I should sell my fancy car and buy an
old red hooptie.

> *K:* No old red hooptie! Keep Fancy
> Car!

M: Laughing. For you, I'll keep it.

My list would be the same.

You were brave today. You made me
proud.

You tasted so good. Felt so nice.

> *K:* Making me blush.
>
> I tried to be brave. Want to make
> you proud.
>
> And you tasted better and felt even
> nicer!

M: I'm happy you liked the new
things we did.

> *K:* Yes! New things! What are we do-
> ing next?

M: Need to work from early to late
the next couple days.

> *K:* Poop. See-Sweet stuff?

*C-Suite! Stupid autocorrect.

M: Smiling. Yes. See-Sweet

Will be able to text, maybe. Not sure.

K: OK.

M: But we'll do something fun later. I promise.

K: OK.

M: You in bed?

K: Yes.

M: Hot there?

K: Like usual.

M: Tee and cowboy undies?

K: Um... No... Wait...

<image, nude body KZ>

M: !!! I don't know what to say!

K: Laughing. Am I brave?

M: Yes. You are brave.

K: Am I good-looking?

M: Yes. You are very good-looking.

And you are very surprising.

I am proud of you for being so brave.

> K: Happy you are surprised.

> Happy you are proud.

> Your turn? Please?

M: Sure! Wait...

<image, nude body MZ>

> K: You are beautiful. Can we see
> each other for real?

M: Yes, but not too fast. We need to
take our time.

> K: Why take time?

M: Some things are better if you go
slow.

Have to take our time. Trust me.

> K: I trust you. We'll go slow. Hope I
> don't faint first.

M: Laughing. I would wake you with
a kiss!

Like a Fairy Prince(ss).

K: Laughing. That would be great!

M: Got to go.

                              K: So soon?

M: Yes. Have to get ready for work.

I'll text, if I can.

                                    K: OK.

M: Sending kisses to you.

                     K: Now I know what they're like!

                     Tell your boobs that I love them.

M: Laughing. I will. They'll like that.

Goodnight Kissy-Naked-Tasty-
Brave-Surprising-KZ.

                           K: Night MZ!

*

MAZIE

How about that? Full frontal nudity. No prompting required. Given a couple days apart, with just a little bit of fun between. Who knows what might happen next?

Pushing limits or pushing buttons. Decisions, decisions.

Chapter Seven

KAZ

"Baby, you're late this morning! I was getting ready to wake you when you came out your door. You think you'll make it to work on time?"

"Yes, GeeGeema, but I have to hurry."

"Hugs, first, then hurry."

"Sure."

"Why are you so late?"

"Dunno," I shout from the kitchen as I put Preston's food on the floor and get a cup of water. "It's been a long time since I've slept through my alarm. I guess I had a really good night's sleep."

"About time," she replies. "Sleep does more than any medicine. You be careful riding to work. Do good once you get there."

"Yes, GeeGeema. Bye-bye."

"And I love you too!"

*

I ride as fast as I can to the store and arrive sweaty and almost, but not quite, late. I'm wearing my baggiest jeans with the phone in the front pocket. I'm hoping Mazie will text.

I check the job list. Restock. Yes! Inside, where it's cool and I can take my time.

Restock isn't all easy. You have to move and break open the heavy boxes and cases, scan inventory, and shift things on the shelves so the new stuff goes in the back. I hate it when customers reach past what's in front! I'll be straightening displays, answering about a million questions for shoppers, and cleaning up any messes little kids make. Doing price checks too. I'll be busy, for sure.

I recheck the list and see that Angel has written herself in every one of her shifts for Carts and Parking Lot. I smile. Sarah must be throwing a whole bunch of spare change out there!

*

A couple hours later, I'm at mangos and peaches, checking for softness, bruises, and shifting stock.

"Excuse me, please."

I turn to find Mazie, standing right next to me, dressed in black, except instead of a T-shirt, jeans, and boots, she's wearing an untucked man-tailored shirt with the two top buttons undone and a mid-thigh skirt. In her high heels, she's taller than me.

"I...I..."

Her black eyes dance. She smiles, red lipstick parting to show her teeth—no gums. She is so beautiful.

She straightens her back ever so slightly and nods her approval when I follow along.

"Can you tell me where the sweet pickles are?"

"I, uh."

"Are you all right, dear?" She touches my shoulder.

It's like electricity. "Yeah. All right. Who?"

"Sweet pickles?" Her whole face is laughing.

"Sweet pickles," I repeat. My brain starts working, sort of. "The middle of aisle five," says my mouth on automatic pilot.

"Yes. I was over there but must've missed them. Could you show me, please?"

I take the lead with her heels click-clicking on the floor a half-step behind. As we round the cap at the end of breads, I see Mr. Amolsch looking at us, or her, from frozen foods on the far side of the store.

"Mazie!" I say under my breath. "What are you doing here?"

She giggles, talking low. "Buying pickles, my sweet. You sure are cute in your apron. You should wear it with no shirt and no jeans so I could run my hands all over your good-looking back and down around your pretty boy-butt!"

I slide into full-blush mode. I feel like I might faint.

Still whispering, "Or I could lift my skirt and let you do the same to my boy-butt. No undies!" Then, in a normal voice, "Why, here they are. I walked right past them." She looks at me, tilts her head, and raises her eyebrows. "Do you know which ones are sweetest?"

"The sweetest? I'm not sure, ma'am."

She reaches past me to pick a jar and whispers. "I'm sure that *you're* the sweetest when you call me ma'am!" She looks at the label for a moment. "I think these will do."

I almost flinch when she reaches out and touches my right arm.

"Thanks for your help!" Another bright smile. Then she turns and walks toward the registers. I think, maybe, she's swinging her own pretty boy-butt a little bit more than she needs to.

As I turn to head back to mangos and peaches, Mr. Amolsch comes around the cap. He stands, swiveling his head to watch her go by, then walks to me.

"Who was that, Kaz?"

"I don't know, Mr. Amolsch," I lie. "Not seen her before."

"Sort of familiar. Sweet pickles, huh?" He looks at me, chews on his lower lip, raises his own eyebrows, and widens his eyes. "Saaa-weeet pickles." He walks away without noticing my blush, then turns. "Kaz, how about you do me a favor and mop that section of the floor? It's a little sticky right there."

*

MAZIE

I laugh all the way back to my car. I've not had that much fun in I don't know how long. Kaz was so calm before she saw me, then totally discombobulated. My teasing left her helpless in those first few minutes. For a moment, it looked as if she would faint. That would've made the whole thing perfect.

And the big guy. The boss? Staring like I was a side of beef.

I sit in my car, laughing as I replay the incident in my head, and watch a cute little redhead wrangle carts. Too curvy.

Plus, as a little extra bonus, as I back out of my parking spot, I roll right over where I killed Chunky Dude. He was the one who kept me from buying these sweet pickles in the first place!

*

Bzz...

> *K:* Are you crazy, coming to the store
> like that?!

M: Laughing. You should've seen your face.

> *K:* Not funny.

M: Did you like my outfit?

> *K:* You were beautiful. But still not
> funny.

M: I wanted to see where you worked.

> *K:* Not funny. Almost fainted.

M: You REALLY blushed!

Probably went all the way to your
pretty tummy!

K: Not funny. At all.

M: Laughing more. Not even a little
funny?

K: OK... A little funny.

M: Better. That's my Blushing-KZ.

K: Never thought I'd see you there.

You almost gave me a heart attack!

M: Laughing.

K: OK. Me too. Laughing.

Were you telling the truth?

M: About what?

K: The skirt. Not wearing any undies.

M: Hardly ever wear undies.

K: !!! True?

M: True. Try it. Like sleeping naked!

K: It was so embarrassing.

You talking about touching my back

and boy-butt.

M: Embarrassing? Why?

K: Somebody might hear!

M: Sigh. Kaz. Everyone's in their own car.

Just us. Be brave. Remember?

K: I'm sorry. Yes, I remember. It's hard.

I thought you were busy at work.

M: Took a break to surprise my KZ.

K: I was surprised, for sure.

Boss wanted to know who you were.

M: The big guy?

K: Yes.

M: He sure gave me the eye.

What did you tell him?

K: That I didn't know.

M: Smart-KZ. Fibbing like that.

Where you at?

K: Home. In my room.

M: Hot?

K: Not too bad.

M: Naked?

K: Too early for bedtime.

M: Still could be naked.

K: Others are here.

GeeGeema and I are going for ice
cream.

M: You driving?

K: Sure! You know I love to drive.
Don't do it often.

I have to pay for gas when I drive for
myself.

If I take the car, I have to explain
everything.

When I ride my bike, I just hop on
and go.

They must think I can't get into any
trouble on my bike.

M: Little do they know…

Am I trouble?

> *K:* I don't understand.

M: Would you be in trouble if they
knew about me?

> *K:* They'd ask lots of questions,
> that's for sure.

M: Think so?

> *K:* Yes. Lots and lots of questions.

M: Should we keep me a secret for a
while?

So, there are no questions?

> *K:* That's probably a good idea.

M: OK. You know best.

> *K:* Gotta go! GeeGeema won't wait
> for ice cream.

M: I wouldn't wait either!

But take undies off, first.

> *K:* Couldn't.

M: People won't know. Just us.

We're brave. Right?

                    K: Right. We're brave.

M: My Brave-Undie-less-KZ!

Have fun!

*

KAZ

"You all right, baby?"

"What do you mean, GeeGeema?"

"You were walking kind of funny."

"You sure see a lot of things for somebody who can't see!"

"Who says I can't see?"

"The doctors. Mom. Dad. You!"

"Doctors?" She dismisses them with a wave of the hand. "And your folks are too busy to know."

"What about you?"

"Well, I'm a liar." She smiles. "We both already know that."

We're sitting in the car, eating our ice cream. Soft serve, really, because that's what we like best. We could use the drive-thru, but GeeGeema insists we go inside "to get some exercise." I think it's so she can trade stories with the older ladies behind the counter.

She always gets the same thing: A medium chocolate sundae made with chocolate-vanilla twist ice cream and no peanuts but lots of chocolate jimmies. Can't get enough chocolate. She always asks for a long spoon.

I switch it up, but I always get it in a cup because Gee-Geema eats whatever I don't, and she can't see to handle a cone. There's usually extra from me because I almost always get brain-freeze. Something I've been told many times that my granddaddy with the cowlick also suffered from. I wish being rich ran in the family!

I shift in my seat. This not wearing undies thing must take some getting used to. I feel a blush coming on and take a mouthful of sundae to cool me down.

"You're awful quiet tonight," GeeGeema says.

"Just thinking."

"What about?"

"Nothing, really. Just thinking."

"Just thinking about nothing? You should be in politics." A grin. "You doing better over your friend?"

"Yeah. I still get sad, but like you said, he wouldn't want me moping around."

"Anything going on?" she asks.

I tell her about work and how Sarah's putting coins in the parking lot to keep Angel working outside.

"She the one you said had the red hair?"

"Angel? Yeah."

"What else?"

I think of Mazie and want to mention her but there'd be too many questions. Instead, I talk about a lady in black who came into the store looking for sweet pickles. I leave out all the dirty stuff, of course, but include the part with Mr. Amolsch watching her leave. That makes her laugh.

"'Saaa-weeet pickles!' That's funny. Men are all alike."

Then, she peers at me. I swear she sees everything.

"I know you have to choose." It's something she hardly ever mentions. "Not like me who never had a choice."

There's a moment of silence.

"If you had to choose, would you be a woman again?"

"Now...there's a question."

"Would you?"

She sighs. "Kaz, being a woman gives you things. Being a man gives you things. Most of those things are the same, or two sides of the same coin. Oh, I suppose being a man has some advantages, but so does being a woman. I've done every single thing I've ever wanted in my life. Only some of them had to do with being a woman. As far as love goes... Nowadays people are more accepting of men and women being with their own, but it's always been going on. Only it was in hiding. It's better to have that out in the open. Doesn't hurt anybody if there's honesty.

"And there's always been people like you, but who never had a choice and ended up the wrong way 'round. Women that were men and men that were women. I once lived in a place where every year at Hallowe'en, the mayor dressed up like a harlot." She gives me the side eye. "For twenty years. A harlot. Now that makes a body wonder."

"But would you ever want to be a man?"

Her voice goes soft. "When I was young, I would've liked to been stronger. I would've liked to have sung down deep. I would've liked to have been more footloose. I would've liked to have had babies without carrying them. I would've liked to have lived without the fear women have of men they don't trust. Now that I'm old, I don't know if any of that matters." She looks at me, this time with sadness in her eyes. "I guess I'm not smart enough to answer your questions. I'm sorry."

"Don't be sorry, GeeGeema, you're always plenty smart and you answered them just fine. Here, you have my extra ice cream."

"Thank you, baby."

*

SK'DOO

I'm looking at Pond but staying far enough away from both Ezme and Pat that neither can speak to me.

All I've been doing is thinking about Pat being in Pond. I don't know how he got there and need to figure out why.

There has never been a Dead in Pond. Ever. But now there is. I somehow missed this burial. I don't know how, but it's true.

I didn't see the gravediggers put Pat in Pond. How can that be? I've been at every other burial. Watched every one, from close or far. Every one. But not this one.

Could the gravediggers have done it the last night there was lightning? If I was in Haven, I would miss it. They buried Deads in the dark, before, when many became that way with illness and there were too many to bury in the day. But this isn't like that.

And how did Pat get so far out in Pond? I don't see machine marks on the ground, and the machines can't go on the water, like me. So, they'd be in the water. But they would still leave tracks getting to Pond.

The gravediggers carried and put Pat so far out in the water? At night? When I was in Haven because of the lightning? Quicks don't like lightning any more than I do—they run from it!

I remember when I checked and old Edge was still there. New Edge appeared between then and now. That's when Pat was buried in Pond. Maybe I didn't know because it happened outside of old Edge and I couldn't know until Edge moved.

I don't how it happened, when it happened, or why it happened. But it happened. That I know!

Chapter Eight

KAZ

It's been two days since I've heard from Mazie and it's making me crazy. I keep jumping because I think I feel my phone buzzing, but it's not.

I've ridden through Eastdale so many times that I'm starting to know who's buried where. I'm sitting on the bench near Jimmy's grave when I check the phone one last time, then, because I'm mad, turn it off.

Why isn't she texting me?

I know why. She's busy doing her bajillionaire C-Suite junk or triple-acrostic whatevers in ink, and I'm sitting here on a stupid bench in a stupid cemetery surrounded by stupid squirrels.

I sigh. I have no idea why she even bothers with me. She's so perfect and I'm so...me.

"Jimmy," I say aloud, like I've been prodded into speaking, "Jimmy, I'm spending time with a person named Mazie who was driving the car that killed you. It makes me feel really weird doing that, and I hope it's okay. With you, I mean.

"I like her so much. She makes me laugh and thinks I'm cute. Yeah, I don't know why either, but she does. She's pretty. You'd think so too, but you'd probably think her boobs were too small. But that doesn't mean you're an idiot."

I lower my voice to a whisper, even though there's nobody in sight. "I touched her boobs, Jimmy. And she kissed me. Real kisses too. My heart beat so fast.

"I hope you don't mind me telling you. I had to tell somebody and you're the only one I have. You were the best at keeping secrets. I guess you really are, now.

"I wish you were here and we could talk for real. Gee-Geema says that as long as I remember, you're never gone. Maybe that's true. But I miss your goofy smile and your stupid jokes. And I miss you too."

I sit a little longer, sort of waiting to cry. But it's only a few tears. Maybe I'm starting to accept that I'll never see my friend again.

*

SK'DOO

"You call that music?"

"I will never love him the way he does me."

"Just shut the hell up, willya?"

I'm near Kazabee as soon as I notice her and beside her the instant her lightning-box stops.

Anger. Confusion. She's unsure. I recognize those feelings. I reach out, just a little, to see if I can get her to talk. I know that helps settle what some Quicks feel.

And she does! To Dead Jimmy who is not far away. I hear her voice. It's not sure, and I feel the same thing inside of her. Then a sort of feeling of fun. Something I'm not sure of, like when I discovered Edge had moved and everything was new-new.

Then, a feeling I know. I don't have a name for it. It's what I feel about lightning-boxes and not being able to sit at burials. Like when the sexton moved away and took the children and Jigs, the dog, or when horses were replaced by machines. I cannot name it, but I know the way she feels.

I know.

*

Bzz...

> *M:* Hey, good looking!

>> *K:* Where have you been? I was so
>> worried!

> *M:* Why? Told you I'd be busy for a
> couple of days.

>> *K:* I missed you.

> *M:* Good.

>> *K:* You miss me?

> *M:* Certainly. You working, tomor-
> row?

>> *K:* In the morning. I'm done at noon.

> *M:* Perfect. Are your toenails
> trimmed?

>> *K:* ??? My toenails are *always*
>> trimmed! Why?

> *M:* Never you mind.

> Meet you at the cemetery, tomorrow
> at 1.

> At the bike rack.

K: Where are we going?

M: At The Bike Rack At One. OKAY?

K: Yes. Sorry. OK. May I ask where
we're going?

M: Someplace trimmed toenails look
best.

Night-night, Curious-KZ. Kisses!

K: Mazie?

Mazie?

Chapter Nine

KAZ

Mazie arrives right on time, as usual. I hop in Fancy Car. As soon as I shut the door, she grabs my shirt, pulls me over, and gives me a kiss. That makes me smile. We turn left out of the cemetery, and she zooms northward.

As soon we're up to speed, she tugs on my tee. "Off."

I happily comply.

Mazie runs her hand along my tummy, up to my face, petting me all over as she goes.

"You're pretty today, Kaz."

"Thank you, Mazie!"

"What have you been doing while we've been apart? Besides missing me, that is."

"I looked up that triple acrostic thing."

"Poetry," she corrects. "Triple acrostic poetry. What do you think?"

"If you can do that kind of stuff, in ink, in different languages, then you're smarter than anybody else I know."

"All it takes is practice, Kaz. It's hard at first, like riding a bike, but after a while, you catch on and cruise along."

"If you say so. I tried looking you up too."

She looks at me, sharply. "What did you find?"

"Nothing. There was no Mazie Maddington anywhere on the Internet that was you. Like no results. At all."

"Wonderful. That's the way I want it."

"But I couldn't find anything on you!"

She laughs. "I spend good money to have myself scrubbed from the web. I'm glad it doesn't go to waste."

"You can do that?"

"Sure. Pay enough and you vanish." She snaps her fingers. "Just like that—poof!"

"Why?"

"C-Suites want to know about people they encounter, especially in negotiations. They think it gives them the upper hand. Not being on the Internet gives me an advantage. I know they're not going to find anything with a casual search. And I know if they know something about me, they had to dig. Knowing that gives me an advantage too."

"I'm not sure I understand."

"You don't have to." She smiles at me. "I looked you up too, after you told me about your dysphoria. I was curious about what I'd find. There isn't much recent stuff under your name."

"I quit using social media."

"Smart not-girl. Only idiots use that crap. But I did find you when I searched the town. You're the 'unnamed teen-ager' in all those news stories I saw, aren't you? School board meetings. Uproar among dumb-shit parents. That was about you, right?"

"Yeah," I mutter. "About me."

"I imagine 'unnamed teenager' isn't the best cover when it comes to remaining unnamed, is it?

"No. Everyone knew it was me."

"You mean everyone in your Podunk town knew it was you." She holds up a finger and twirls it. "Wahoo. Big flippin' deal. Get a few miles out and nobody has the faintest idea."

"I guess."

"I'm sure, Kaz. It's a bad idea to allow that kind of stuff to get to you. It's posted, but it doesn't contain your name, so there's not much you can do about it. It might bother you, but at least it's accurate. Well, at least not lies. And there's not much posted with your name, not that I found."

I drop my voice. "They called me 'fag-dyke' and 'she-male' and 'he-she' and stuff like that. Some of the parents were worse than their kids; said I was trying to turn people to sin, that I was evil and God hated me and I was going to hell. Some even made death threats. Mom and Dad started a couple lawsuits and stopped that. It still hurts."

"Good for Mom and Dad. And I'm sure it does hurt. But there's no stopping idiots from being idiots. Especially religious idiots, bless their hearts. The best thing is to stay the hell off social media. It'll eat you alive. I don't have active accounts anywhere, personal or professional. And I make enough money to have myself wiped from any place I don't want to appear."

"Must be nice."

"It is. Tell me, am I your secret?"

"I don't understand."

"Kaz, are you keeping me a secret?"

"Yes."

"That gives you power over people who would want to know. And you are my secret and that does the same for me. Would you want everyone to know what we're doing?"

"No."

"The only way to do that is to keep it to ourselves, between us and nobody else. Our business is our business.

Right?"

"Right."

She grabs the hair behind my head and pulls me over for a kiss but not a long enough one because she's driving.

"Want to guess where we're going?"

"No idea."

"Look in the dash."

I open it up and find a pair of expensive sunglasses.

"Put them on."

I do and look at her.

"Very nice. Look there, again."

I pull out something made of tan cloth. Confused, I unfold it. "Boy's board shorts?"

She raises an eyebrow at me. "Don't you know that a boy's different than a male?"

"That I know. It's these shorts I don't understand."

Mazie laughs. "Where do you go with sunglasses and board shorts and toenails that are trimmed?"

I feel my eyes get wide. "The beach? I can't go to the beach!"

She reaches over and pulls me to another kiss. "That's wrong, Brave-Kaz. You can go anywhere." She glances toward the back seat. "Check out the hat."

It's tan. Straw, with a straight brim a couple inches wide.

"Pull your hair back and put it on."

I do as I'm told and get a bright smile.

"Your own GeeGeema wouldn't know you!"

"GeeGeema is almost blind, y'know."

"So is everyone else. That's today's lesson."

"Mazie... Really. I cannot do this."

"Stop saying that, Kaz, or I'll get mad. Out of those jeans and into those shorts."

I toss the hat and glasses in the back and slide my seat the whole way back. The car *bings* three times because my belt's undone.

Kicking my shoes off, I unbutton my jeans and, lifting my butt, wriggle them down to my knees, then push them off my feet.

"Hold on. Kneel on the seat, turned toward me."

I do as I'm told.

She gives me goose bumps by running a finger down the parallel scars on the upper part of my left leg. "Cutting?"

I nod.

"You've stopped that?"

"So far."

She runs her open hand along the outside of my upper leg with her fingers reaching around back. It makes me close my eyes.

"Your legs are absolutely beautiful. All the biking. Nice,

long muscles. So smooth. Do you shave?"

"Don't have to," I stutter.

"Lucky, lucky you." She puts her hand between my knees and bounces it back and forth. "Wider."

I spread my legs as far apart as I can and still stay on the seat. My heart pounds. My stomach muscles contract as she runs her fingers over the front of my undies.

"I was expecting cowboys." Mazie takes the elastic band, pulls it away from my tummy, peeks over the top, looks up at me, and smiles. "Just checking." They snap back when she lets go. Then, she slowly runs the top of her hand, fingernails to wrist, along the bottom-side of the cloth between my thighs.

The feel of it makes me straighten my back and gasp.

"No slouching is good. Fold up those jeans, place them in the back, pull on those shorts, and lose the white socks. You ain't no middle-aged man. Or male, for that matter."

The board shorts confuse me. "What's this mesh inside?"

"To hold your junk. If you had any."

We sit in silence for the rest of the drive. By the time we pull into the parking lot my anxiety is more than maxed out.

"The blacktop will be hot. Wear your shoes. No shirt."

I'm close to hyperventilating. "Mazie. Please don't get mad. But I really-really-really can't do this."

"Kaz," she says calmly as she touches my face. "Kaz. Sweetheart. Look at me. Look at me. This is like when we walked around the car. Remember?"

"No, Mazie. No, it's not. Those people were in cars, these people...they're all over."

"Kaz, look at me." She lightly slaps my cheek. "These people are in cars too"—she taps the side of my head—"in their brains. If they look at you, they won't see who you think you are. They're going to see skinny brown male. With those shorts, hat, and glasses they won't even notice that your armpits are shaved. But nobody's gonna be looking at you, anyway."

"Why not?"

A huge smile. "Because they're all going to be looking at me!"

Getting out of Fancy Car is one of the bravest things I've ever done. Maybe even braver than telling Mom and Dad I was stuck. But Mazie's right. From the moment she removes her shirt and starts sliding out of her jeans, I am invisible.

I stand at the back of Fancy Car, naked from the waist up, but receive nothing but uninterested glances. All eyes are on her.

When she comes back to pop the trunk, I see why. With her beautiful face, no-line tan, long legs, toned muscles, gold bracelet, and four-tiny-white-triangle bathing suit, she leaves me breathless.

"Wow. Mazie. I don't know what to say."

She ignores my compliment. "Grab the beach chairs. And here, carry these too." She hands me two big white towels. "And this—" She slips the strap of a white beach bag into my hands. "You know why you're carrying all that stuff?"

"Because you told me to?"

She laughs. "No, it's because you're the lucky fellow with the prettiest girl on the beach. Attend, slave."

I follow her flip-flops, trying not to stare too much at her narrow waist, back dimples, and swaying boy-butt. How does that suit stay on?

Heads swivel, but I know nobody's looking at me, except, maybe, to wonder why I'm with her.

We don't go all the way to the water but set up in the shade of a tree where the grass turns to sand. She points to where she wants the chairs. Makes me move them, twice. Tells me to drape them with the towels, then loudly scolds me for not doing it right.

By the time she's done with me, those around us are looking at me with pity in their eyes.

We sit. Mazie slides her feet from her flips. "Take off your shoes." She leans to look at my feet and nods. "Nails nicely trimmed." Then looks at me. "Your feet are bigger than mine, but not too bad, considering your height."

"Gee. Thanks."

"You're probably less tippy than me." She leans back in her chair and sighs. "Isn't this nice?" She stretches her perfect legs and wiggles her perfect toes. Then she looks at me. "How you getting along, skinny brown not-male?"

"Okay. I'm breathing normal again." I try to catch my look in the reflection of her shades.

She shows her teeth. "Don't worry, Kaz. You know you're doing good 'cause you're hangin' with me! And, incidentally, I'm nearly dead from thirst. Get me a bottle of water from the bag. You should've offered me one the moment we sat down! You may have one, if you wish."

After several minutes, I'm starting to feel okay with what's happening around me.

"We going in?"

"In the water? Are you insane? It's filthy. Highest bacteria count so far this summer. Easy to look that up, yet all these idiots are swimming." She adjusts her sunglasses. "I'm uncomfortable being in the wind that blows across it. You should be happy I managed to be here."

I can't tell if she's joking.

"Besides, it'd ruin my look, and if you got wet up to your waist your cover might be blown." She glances at my crotch. "You got a dent where a bump should be."

"Oh. Yeah."

"Not that I have faith any of these stupes around us would notice." She looks at me. "So, what's today's lesson?"

"Always listen to Mazie?"

A laugh and a reach to pet my face.

I lean back.

"Why are you dodging my public display of affection?"

"Because I'm afraid..."

"...somebody might see." She finishes for me. "Let me show you something." She hooks two fingers over my collarbone, pulls me to her, and kisses me on the lips. "There. Did the world end?"

"Uh. No."

She pretends to wipe something off my chest, skittering across my nipples as she goes. "How about now?"

I smile. "World's still here."

"I could sit behind you, hold you so you couldn't move, stick my tongue in your ear, bite your neck, jam my hand down your crotch, and rub you from one orgasm to the next, and the world *still* wouldn't end. What do you think about that?"

"I think we should make sure that's true."

Another laugh. I like that.

"Since you're being such a good sport, Kaz, and are mildly entertaining, I shall give you a free lesson in people watching."

"People watching?"

"My dear, the most valuable of skills one might culti-vate." She waves a hand in front of us. "Take a look around, Learner-Kaz, and tell me what you see."

"People."

She gives me the side-eye and a sigh. "No. Wrong. What you see are idiots. All this lovely and varied flesh and what are the idiots doing?" She hunches over, holds her hands to-gether in front of her face, and moves her thumbs. "Looking at their phones. From now on out, nothing but generation after generation of hunchbacked idiots. God, how I hate people who slouch."

She looks at me and I sit up.

Mazie smiles. "Lessons begin: See this jock coming out of the water? Watch how he stands straighter and sticks out his chest as he passes. It's called 'preening behavior.' He's trying to impress me and make you look less desirable. Al-most everybody does the same sort of thing, no matter what they are, or what they're chasing. Most don't even know they're doing it."

"They don't know they do it?"

"Well, some do, and are good at it. Mostly, it's idiots who make a real show of it. Can you see any?"

"This person with muscles wearing the blue briefs?"

"'Person with muscles?'" She mocks. "Honestly, Kaz.

Has it come to that?"

"I don't want to assume..."

She interrupts. "Assume? If you see a red car in a parking lot, do you *assume* it's red?"

"No, but..."

"Let's say you see that same car, but with the door open, and there's blue paint on the door frame. Then, what do you *assume*?"

"That it's a repaint. That it's red now, but it was blue."

"Very good. Let's say the repaint is perfect in every way." Mazie stretches in her chair. "What color is the car?"

"Red."

"That *person* with muscles is like the car before you open the door, or the car with the perfect paint job. The car is red. The person with muscles is male. A man. That's not an assumption, that's a conclusion based on available evidence."

"Cars are things. People aren't things!"

She laughs. "If somebody announced a storm was on its way and that every *thing* on this beach would be blown away, would you be safe because you're not a thing?"

"No."

"Correct. If our muscleman tells me he prefers a particular pronoun, then, fine. Otherwise, I'm not torturing a language I love to make it fit a possibility that might not exist.

You may, if you wish, but do not expect me to play along. Understand?"

"Yes. I understand."

"At this moment, what do others conclude about you?"

"That I'm male."

"What if I change your paint job with a bikini top?"

"That I'm female."

"The conclusion changes with the evidence. Yes?"

"I guess. Yes."

"We're lucky that way."

"I never thought I was lucky."

"You only consider the problem, not the advantage. We may present any way we wish. For example, I could bind my small and perfect breasts, get myself a butch haircut, masculine clothes, walk with my shoulders instead of my hips, and drop my voice a notch. To the rest of the world, I would be a man kissing you. On the other hand"—she nods at a large bearish person—"he looks like he looks no matter what he has to be. So, you see, we're lucky.

"Now how about you pick somebody else, Kaz. Who else is making a show of themselves?"

"Um, that blonde coming out onto shore?"

"And now we're avoiding pronouns. I am astonished that you assumed she's blonde, but there you go. Arms up, twisting her hair to get rid of the filthy, bacteria-laden water.

Showing off her large breasts, narrow waist, baby capable hips, and long legs. Underside of her arms too. An erogenous zone for many and a near-universal sign of submission for females."

It's like Mazie's dissecting a frog.

"Ventral arm display may also indicate a person that is without fear in, is unaware of, or is ignoring the dangers within their environment, especially for a male—similar to them standing or walking with their hands behind their backs. I will concede that the blonde *is* kind of tasty. But it appears she's wasting her time because everyone else is looking at their goddam phone."

She points. "Here's an out-of-shape guy wearing lots of gold because there's more than one way to bait a trap. Here's a girl covered with tats. Another kind of lure."

"Lots of people have tattoos. Would you ever get one?"

She turns to me and smiles. "Look at me, Kaz. I mean, *look at me*. What could possibly be added to make me more perfect?" Back to the crowd. "And here's yet another strutting muscle boy in a sweet pickle sling. I cannot understand why guys want to show off their junk unless they're trolling for another like them." She looks at me over the top of her glasses. "Ever see a guy's junk?"

"Not really." I blush.

"In porn, then. Do you like what's done with it?"

Full blush mode.

"Oh, Kaz, you are so beautiful when you blush like that. All the way down to your sweet tummy!" She pats it with her hand.

"Mazie!"

She looks at me. No smile. "Always remember that porn's fake. It takes things that aren't that good and makes them look better. Like a guy's junk. In porn, it looks pretty good. In real life"—she shakes her head and frowns—"all I see is grumpy toads."

I look down the beach for another idiot but instead see a familiar red ponytail bouncing our way. "Oh, my God!"

"What's wrong?"

"It's Angel. From work. Angel."

Mazie puts her hand on mine. "Cool your jets. Where away?"

"To the left. Red hair. Green two-piece."

"The parking lot girl?" A sigh. "I love real redheads. You'll be fine," she says calmly. "Just sit still, look out at the water, and don't turn your head."

"She's gonna know who I am!"

"Wrong. She knows you as a sweet-pickle-shelving, not-girl-not-boy weirdo wearing a blue shirt and an apron. What on earth makes you think that she's perceptive enough to see you as a skinny brown male in a hat and shades attending a goddess?"

I hold my breath as Angel walks past, glances our way, and continues on, phone in hand.

"See that, Kaz? Nothing to it. With that pale skin she must be wearing, what, SPF Ten Thousand? What color are her eyes?"

"I don't know."

"Shame on you. She is a sweet little number."

"I guess she is pretty cute."

"I like her freckles. Did you notice how she bounced a bit more when she was in your field of view?"

"She did?"

"Yep. Sexy-Kaz," Mazie singsongs. "Pullin' in the red-heads!"

We sit a while longer.

"Who's in charge here?"

"You," I reply.

"Thank you, but I mean with all this back and forth between females, nonbinaries, and males. Who's in charge?"

"I never thought about it."

"Exactly why I'm asking. Who do you think is in charge?"

"I don't know."

"When Bouncy Red performed those extra body motions to get your attention, who was in charge?"

"She was?"

"Are you asking me or telling me?"

"Telling you. She was in charge."

"Correct. And let's pretend you were actually smart enough to notice those motions and ignored them or acted upon them. Who would be in charge then?"

"Me. So it's trading. Going back-and-forth."

"Yes. Some people either miss the chance to trade or don't notice the attempt to trade." Mazie looks at me and continues. "Socially awkward people: nerds, geeks, dorks, dweebs, and so forth are in that category."

"Like me."

"Yes, but you're learning how not to be one of them and that earns you extra points. Some people think they can choose not to be involved in any part of any trade, or think they are above it." She smiles. "But they're not smart enough to understand that is an impossibility. And then you have the idiots who try to force a trade or ignore the fact that it's not their turn to trade. There are times when idiots try to take what you don't want them to have. Do you know what I'm talking about?"

"Yeah. Rape and like that."

"Happens to everybody, especially the 'and like that' part. It's why you need to be fast, smart, and strong."

"To fight?"

She nods at a person who's big and looks strong. "What could you do if he grabbed you?"

"Maybe yell. Could you fight them off?"

"Yelling's a good start, but since I'm smart, I'd spot him and avoid trouble. If it came down to a mental battle, I'd clean his clock. A physical altercation might be interesting. I'm not sure I could inflict enough damage, but I'd try." She smiles at me. "We'd let the doctors decide who won."

"Like me breaking that guy's nose."

Mazie nods. "Yes. He was trying to take something valuable. You responded in a manner your parents, GeeGeema, and I think was reasonable. The trick is to learn to shut those idiots down before you reach the point of nose-breaking. Y'know, you should learn to box. Real boxing, not that fake exercise stuff. Long arms like yours? Good jab and a cross? Nobody'd stand a chance." She changes the subject. "What do you think of everybody seeing your not-boobs?"

"I sort of forgot about it."

"You do understand it has nothing to do with being female, nonbinary, or male?"

"It doesn't?"

"No. It's where we're at. What's a topless beach?"

"Where everyone can wear only a bottom."

"Yes. I could be sitting here, just like you, with my boobs hanging out. Nobody would care. Shit...it's likely nobody would even notice because, like I told you before, idiots like big ones."

"You've been to topless beaches?"

"Sure. Clothing optional and nude beaches too, where you can wear nothing. But I don't like those as much. Clothing optional and you get too many cowardly crotch-and-boob-oglers who come to stare and take photos when they think you're not looking. Nude beaches." She shakes her head. "Too many grumpy toads!"

We stay another hour, talking about the people going by. Angel strolls past a couple more times, once with some of her friends from school. Those who aren't on their phones glance or outright stare at Mazie but pay very little attention to me.

As the shade from the tree moves away from us, she declares she's tired of smelling all the burning flesh and fat. I am told to fold the towels and the chairs, pick up the beach bag, and carry it all back to the car.

Once there, she takes the towels and bag from me. The bag goes on the back seat. I put the chairs in the trunk. She motions me to the driver's side, tosses me a towel, and shows me how to drape it over the car seat before sitting. I'm curious, but don't ask why because I figure she probably won't tell me.

*

MAZIE

"What did Student-Kaz learn today?"

"People see what they want to see?"

"Are you asking me or telling me?"

"Telling you. I learned that people see what they want to see."

"Anything else?"

"People do things they don't know they're doing, and you can spot the fakers who overdo it."

"Does it matter if they are female, nonbinary, or male?"

Kaz shakes her head. "No."

"What else?"

"Power is traded but you have to be ready for when it's not."

I smile. "And what did you learn about yourself, Kaz?"

"I'm braver than I thought. What I think I am isn't the same as what others see. That I should learn to box, and"—a grin—"...that I think Angel is kind of cute."

The car *bings* three times as I unbuckle my seatbelt, get up on my knees, and kiss her on the cheek. "That's my Smart-Kaz. And now, your reward for paying attention."

I reach between the seats, unzip the beach bag, and take out a bottle of moisturizing lotion, expensive, but worth it.

I sit, look at Kaz, and smile. "Any smart person, female, nonbinary, or male, knows to moisturize their skin after a day in the sun." With that, I remove my top, squirt a dollop into my hand, rub my palms together, and start applying the lotion to my skin.

As expected, the car drifts.

"Eyes on the road, please, Chauffeur-Kaz!"

"I could turn on the autopilot."

"No. You like to drive. So, drive."

Kaz watches out of the corner of her eye as I smooth the lotion around my neck, across my collarbones, shoulders, and down my arms. I hold my shining fingers in front of her nose. "Mmm... Smell. Nice, isn't it?"

Another squirt of moisturizer. Across my chest and breasts, down my ribcage. I arch my back and run my hands there too.

She reaches a hand to touch me.

"Hands on the wheel, Driver-Kaz. Ten and two."

"I was taught three and nine."

"I don't care what time it is. Hands on the wheel."

"Mazie—this isn't fair!"

I laugh. "Almost forgot my boy-butt. It didn't get much sun but it can never be too soft." I recline the seat and lift my hips. I remove the rest of my suit, roll onto my side, and point my bottom right at her. I snake a hand over the small of my back and slide it over, around, and between the cheeks of my ass.

She swerves, but not into the oncoming lane.

I roll onto my back, close my eyes, raise my knees, and part my legs. At this angle, she'll see nothing but the tendons in my groin and a neat dark triangle. All promise, no delivery.

Since Kaz likes my muscles so much, I contract my abs to make them stand out and run slickened hands down the inside of my thighs around my knees and back up the outside. I reverse and reverse again. Then down my legs to my feet.

I look at Kaz who is squirming in frustration.

"You are slowing. Please mind the speed limit!" Reaching into the back of the car, I retrieve a pair of jeans and shimmy into them. "Ha! I told you they'd fit."

She does a double-take. "Hey, those're mine!"

"Not anymore." I pull on my tee, lean over, purposely put my breast against her shoulder, and stick my tongue in her ear.

"Are you *trying* to make me wreck Fancy Car?"

I laugh and hit the autopilot button. "Time for you to get dressed."

I see there's a wet spot on the bottom of her board shorts.

"Mazie. I really need my jeans back!"

"These are mine, now. What's wrong with the ones I am so graciously allowing you to have?"

"They aren't the kind I wear. Mom'll notice."

"You'll have to keep them secret. Like me."

"Mazie..."

I shoot her a stern look and put an edge in my voice. "I could make you go home wearing nothing but those board shorts. You think ol' Mom would notice that?"

She kowtows. "Okay, Mazie, okay!"

*

Bzz...

> *M:* KZ?
>
> KZ?
>
> Come on, KZ.
>
> Look... I *know* you're reading
> these messages.

> > *K:* Just Stop Texting. I'm MAD at
> >
> > you.

> *M:* I was kidding, KZ.

  K: Didn't sound like you were kid-

            ding.

M: Do you really think I'd do that?

Leave you with just the shorts?

Do you really think I'm that mean?

Hurts my feelings, you thinking I'm
that mean.

  K: Sounded like you were that mean.

M: Now, KZ... We're friends, right?

We are friends. Right?

         K: Maybe.

M: Listen to yourself.

Are we 13 and back in middle
school?

Are we?

          K: No.

M: I was kidding around.

Guess I took it too far.

I'm sorry. I apologize. Please forgive
me.

Please? PLEEEEEEZE?

> K: Now *you* sound like you're 13 years old!

M: Smiling. I haven't been 13 in 20 years.

> K: 33? Really???

M: Please, KZ, no cradle-robbing jokes.

> K: Cradle-robbing?

M: Look it up. I'll wait.

> K: Hold on...

M: You having to look up cradle-robbing?

THAT makes me feel like a cradle-robber.

> K: OH! Ick.
>
> You're *not* a cradle-robber. Cause I'm not in a cradle.

M: Thanks.

> K: I don't know how to say this...

M: Just say it.

> *K:* I always thought 33 was old.

M: Wow. Thanks. Feel *way* better,
now!

> *K:* NO! I mean. I didn't think you
> were even late 20s.
>
> You don't have any lines on you...
> Anywhere.

M: Lines, you say. Not wrinkles.
Diplomat-Kaz.

You want to know my secret?

> *K:* Yes!

M: Always moisturize your skin after
a day in the sun.

> *K:* !!! Laughing.

M: Good.

It's nice you looked so carefully to
see no...lines.

> *K:* You kidding? I almost wrecked
> Fancy Car!
>
> Wanted to touch you so bad.

Not being able to... Grrr...

Probably will dream of you.

M: Not touching is part of the fun.
Dreaming = Good.

K: I was all wet and not from the
beach.

M: Laughing.

You know how to take care of that,
right?

K: I suppose. Would be better with
you.

M: Thank you. Send pictures?

K: I am not that un-mad at you!

M: Laughing.

More See-Sweet stuff for couple of
days.

Have to make money for my next
Fancy Car!

No texting, for sure.

K: OK. Will you visit the store? Skirt
with no undies?

M: Laughing. No. Will be away.

Washington D.C.

> *K:* Wow. Important.

M: Not as important as you!

Thank you for forgiving me.

> *K:* You're welcome.

M: Have to get packed for my
travels.

Goodnight, Sweet-KZ.

> *K:* Night!

M: Will miss you, dear heart.

Be sure to attend to your wetness
problem.

> *K:* Mazie = Ornery.

M: Kaz = Hornery!

> *K:* Grrr... Night!

*

MAZIE

Well, that was fun. Kaz handled the stress at the beach far

better than I thought she would.

I love putting myself on display like that. Having her with me made it so much better. Taught her some much-needed social skills. She'll put them to good use. As smart as she is, she could do anything she wanted, if only she was more self-confident.

Frustrated the hell out of her the way home, that's for certain. Maybe pushed a little too hard with the threat to expose her to ol' mom. But talking her into forgiving me wasn't difficult. That's what counts, along with her knowing to not contradict me.

I like having a pair of her jeans. A trophy of sorts. Stolen. Taken against her will. Seeing Kaz in mine, and how well she fit them, was almost more than I could stand.

*

Packing for travel is almost automatic. I always take the same clothes: A severe suit of black armor, in case I run into a self-important badass who thinks they can outmaneuver me. And a more colorful sexy-babe costume for the idiots who are distracted by flesh. It takes surprisingly little for that to happen: a hint of cleavage, a little thigh, a whiff of a promise of more. It's amazing how some of the rich and powerful allow items as insignificant as tits and ass to grease the skids.

Even my suit of armor shows a little skin for the appreciative warrior. It's tailored in such a way that a lean over the negotiating table reveals a tantalizing peek down the front of the blazer. I don't have much on top, but what I have is choice.

And my golf togs. I smile. This deal, with these particular people, there will be at least a couple of rounds. I hope those involved have sharpened their short game. I don't mind losing on purpose somewhere close to par, but giving up a dozen strokes in a convincing manner to an idiot who couldn't sink a putt into a bathtub is damned difficult. A girl can hook and slice and blame it on the rented clubs only so many times!

I check the time. A few more minutes until I need to leave. I walk around my place before I go, making sure everything is where it should be.

There, sitting on glass shelves, is my growing collection of paperweights. I can't visit my real trophies, so I consider their weights as avatars. Each represents an entry on my list.

Like them, each is carefully described and recorded. And like them, each is unique in size, color, and pattern. The last one purchased is a finely swirled combination of rich blues and greens to remind me of the pond.

I wonder what paperweight would be appropriate for Kaz. She'll never have one, of course, but were I searching...

I remember back to when I first started collecting. I saw a weight that fascinated me: a frozen bubble of air, tied into a knot and suspended in clear, light-green glass. It didn't match the subject I wanted to represent, so I passed it by. Were I buying for Kaz, I would search to find one like it.

Time to go. I hope the idiots in security are working more efficiently than usual. The flight isn't usually crowded, but God, how I hate to fly!

Chapter Ten

KAZ

I get to work the next day and find I'm assigned to Carts and Parking Lot. Must be Angel's day off.

Crap. It's only supposed to be 98 percent humidity and a million-billion degrees in the shade, and there isn't any shade out in the parking lot. I put on some sunscreen from the bottle Mr. Amolsch provides for us. Images of Mazie and her shiny, lotion-covered skin flash through my mind.

It's a super-busy day. I grumble about the idiots leaving carts in the middle of wherever; grumble while I pick their garbage up from the hot blacktop, and grumble while I fight the bees flying around the trash cans. I'm uncomfortable near the section where Jimmy died, but instead of crying, I sort of push it out of my mind and get on with what I'm doing.

Five hours later I am wiped out. I push my last load of carts into the store, shove them into their slot, and lean against them.

Sarah looks at me from her register. "My God, Kaz, you look like you're ready to pass out."

"It's hot." I use my sweaty T-shirt sleeve to wipe my sweaty face. "Like hot-hot. Like melt your shoes hot. But I'm done. It's my last day for the week. Y'know, I gotta give Angel credit. That's some tough work right there."

"She says she's lost ten pounds doing it. And has found twelve dollars and eighty-seven cents in change."

"She's keeping count, huh? I didn't find anything."

Sarah gives me a fake frown. "That's my fault. Tell you what. Grab a bottle of water in the back and I'll buy. Deal?"

I nod. "Yeah. Deal. Thanks. Cold water is better than money."

I walk slowly to the back. On the way, I'm asked where the breadsticks are, where the gluten-free foods are, and am told to tell the manager that the store is out of frozen banana smoothies and all we have left are frozen pineapple smoothies and that some people are allergic to pineapple.

Fine.

I grab a bottle of water from the cooler, sit in one of the lunch chairs, and lean my head back against the cement-block wall. It's not pretty, but it's cool. I crack the bottle open and chug about half.

"Kaz," Mr. Amolsch warns as he walks in from the front, "don't drink too much cold water all at once; it can give you cramps. Make you sick."

"Yeah. Okay."

"Hot out there, huh?"

"Hot? Not sure if that's the word for it. A person asked me to tell you that we're out of frozen banana smoothies."

He chuckles and holds up a big hand. "Let me guess. She's allergic to pineapple, right? Thanks, but she caught me. It's like they think I don't track the inventory. With it as hot as it's been, that frozen smoothie stuff has been flying out of the freezers. Um...something was delivered for you today."

"For me?"

"Yeah. Sort of odd. Were you expecting anything?"

I shake my head.

"Well, anyway, here it is." He plunks a lumpy envelope on the table. I can tell he wants to know what it is.

"Thank you, Mr. Amolsch." I look at him the way Mazie does when she wants me to shut up.

"Yeah. No problem." He turns and leaves.

Wow. I'm gonna hafta remember that little trick.

No return address. It's one of those plastic bag things with the bubbles. I struggle to get it open. There's a small, fuzzy jewelry box inside along with a printed note: *For your sweet ears.*

Mazie. Who else could it be? I open the red box and find, sitting in red velvet, a pair of small gold hoop earrings with what looks like a diamond and a round garnet. Wow.

I gulp the rest of my water and ride home. Once I've showered, I look them up and find them in a number of online stores. Kind of expensive. Fourteen-carat gold and those are real diamonds. The red stones are rubies! They're not big and flashy, and you might not even notice them. But they'd look good on anybody. They're perfect. Exactly like something Mazie would pick.

It's been so long since I've worn earrings that only my right earlobe has an open hole. The gold, white, and red look great against my color. I look at it in the mirror, twisting my neck to see, and get a shiver that runs through my whole body. I'll only wear it when I'm outside the house and I absolutely can't wait for Mazie to see it.

I hide the box in the back of my underwear drawer.

*

SK'DOO

"Chocolate is best."

"Of course I fake it. It's the only way I can get them to stop."

"Those French girls sure are pretty."

I follow new Edge from Descher to Pond to rest near Pat and wait until the turtles come out to the sunken tree. I want to try an idea that might let me figure out how he's buried.

"I don't care what anybody says, I don't think she's cute."

"That's too tight!"

"A new phone?"

This Dead sure has a lot to say.

The big turtle climbs from the water onto the log.

I move to it, press against its head and...I'm turtle.

Like before, I decide to suggest and let turtle do the rest.

Into Pond, I think. Then wait. And wait.

Turtle slides into the water. I've never been in water. It pushes up from below.

It's hard to go where we want. Turtle doesn't care much about the direction. We slowly swim across Pond. I feel the familiar tingle of Edge: it's in the water too. I don't think we're fast enough to bump hard enough to hurt, but we'll be careful.

I think which way I want to go. "Down."

I-turtle gulps and we sink.

We run slower as we drop because now we're feel-ing...cold. The light becomes fainter and it's difficult to see.

A large dark object appears, wrapped in cloth.

Pat's like the first Deads. Now I know.

"I like her because she's nice to me."

We somehow smell the water.

I've never smelled water before. That's new-new.

A dim idea of happy comes into my turtle head. Not of Pat, but of the many tiny things wriggling around and in him.

One goes by, too close, and before I can stop, we snap it into our mouth, and I find out what it's like to turtle-eat.

There are other things here. Very fast things. We pay them no attention since we are big enough that they do not bother us.

We spin in a circle. Even though the light is dim I can see there are no machines. Pat was put here without them.

"Are you sure it's okay for us to sit this way?"

Turtle starts drifting. I suggest we get closer, using the feeling of eating to help. It's so hard to go where we want. Our hands and feet move in different directions all at once. I have no idea how to control them. I'm not sure turtle does either.

We see something shiny. I urge us to it.

Eat. I think. *Eat. Eat.* A snap of a mouth, a twist and a pull. We feel a soft *pop* and the object comes free.

Up, Turtle thinks.

Stay, I argue.

Up, Turtle decides.

I had forgotten about breathing. I don't do that.

"Her hands are so warm."

Over to the grass we go.

Turtle wants his spot on the log. *Sleep.*

We manage to drop the shiny just beyond where it could fall back into Pond.

Further, I think.

Sleep.

I've lost all control. We go back to be in the sun, to be warm and to rest. Turtle's thoughts vanish as it slides to sleep.

I slide to look at what we brought from so deep in Pond.

I'm not sure what it is, but it's yellow metal, white, and red.

Chapter Eleven

KAZ

The next afternoon, GeeGeema, Preston, and I are sitting watching an old movie. She can't see the screen but enjoys listening. There's a wheezing fat man who's looking for a bird, I think, and a tough guy who talks like he has something in his mouth. I guess it's better than golf.

"GeeGeema?"

"Yes, baby."

"How many boyfriends did you have?"

She takes the remote, turns down the sound, and stares at me. "What was that?"

"I asked how many boyfriends you had."

"What brings this on?"

"We were talking about it at work," I lie. "And I sort of wondered, you know, about you."

"You've seen those pictures of me, back when I was your age? Tall and pretty. The fellows showed some interest."

"So, you had a lot of boyfriends?

"Oh my, yes. The first one when I was fourteen."

"Fourteen?"

"Things were different back then. Momma and Daddy, they kept a close eye on me. Not like now, with kids running wild. At fourteen, we sat side-by-side in church and could only see each other when there was family around."

"What if you snuck?"

"Snuck? I would've been whipped! And that boy? My daddy would've whipped him good and then sent him home to get whipped by his own daddy."

"You weren't really whipped though, right?"

"Not with a whip, no, but with a leather belt. Get hit a few times on the bottom with that and you paid mind. Wouldn't cut your skin but raised welts and bruises. Bad ones too, if you deserved them. Daddy said he could whip me as long as I lived in his house. But I was mostly good enough that he didn't have to."

"How old were you when you got your first real kiss?"

She raises her eyebrows at me. "My first real kiss, kiss?"

I nod, then have to say, "yes" because she doesn't see me.

"I was seventeen. Stephen Wallace Abernathy Montgomery."

"That's some name."

"He was some kind of fellow. Happened the last week of June. It was just before July Fourth."

"You remember that?"

"If you forget it, it's not your first real kiss!"

"What happened?"

"It was a Saturday. Cool for late June. We were out for a walk where nobody else was. I was letting him hold my hand."

"You were a wild one!"

She laughs. "I was old enough to be on my own. Trusted." Her eyes glitter. "I shouldn't have been. We were holding hands. We stopped walking. We stopped talking. I looked at him. He looked at me." Her face is lost in memories. "And I kissed him."

"GeeGeema—you kissed him?"

"I kissed him hard too." She laughs, suddenly young. "I had to. That man was so shy... If I waited for him, we'd still be standing there!"

"What was he like?"

"Stephen Wallace was tall and thin. Handsome. I never wasted time with any toady-looking fellows. Kind. Smart. Gentle. He had soft green eyes. He was just what I liked. Perfect. I wanted to be with him so bad it made my bones ache."

"Why didn't you marry him?"

"Wanted to but couldn't."

"Couldn't?"

"Too young without my parents' permission. But that wouldn't have mattered, one way or the other."

"Why not?

"He was the wrong color. Or I was. In the state we lived, in lots of states, it was illegal for us to be married. They called them 'miscegenation laws.' Look them up when you want to learn something about the way things were."

"What happened?"

"He was called away to war. Never came back."

"I'm sorry."

"It's okay. That's the way the world is." She smiles a little.

"May I ask you something really personal?"

GeeGeema squeezes my hand. "I know what you want to ask. Stephen Wallace was the first man I was ever with. We were together the week before he left. Neither of us knew what we were doing, and we were plenty awkward at first, but by the end of the week, things were going pretty smooth.

It was wonderful."

"And how old were you?"

"Seventeen, like I told you."

"That's a year younger than me!"

"I always said you were a late bloomer, didn't I?"

"I know, but GeeGeema!"

She laughs, then turns serious. "I...we took an awful chance. Had we been caught..." She shakes her head. "But we loved each other and didn't care what happened. Still, I was relieved when things ran normal the next month. After I got news he was killed, I was sorry I didn't have his baby, as hard as that would've been."

"That's so sad."

"But if Stephen Wallace had come back, or if I'd've had his child, maybe I wouldn't have married who I did and you wouldn't be here with me, would you?" A pause. "There were other fellows after that." She shrugs. "Then I met your great-great-granddaddy. He was okay."

"Just okay?"

"Okay enough to make me forget my sorrow over my Stephen Wallace." She smiles. "We had a good life, he and me." She squeezes my hand again. "But I miss him so, some-times."

I don't know which man she's talking about, the one she married or Stephen Wallace. Both, probably.

I hug her.

"Now. You tell me what really brought this on and no telling stories about work!"

She sees everything, I remind myself for the thousandth time. I take a deep breath. "GeeGeema, can you keep a secret?"

"Nobody listens to me."

"There's this person I met, and I like them very much. We've been spending time together, and..."

"You got kissed?"

I grab her arm and shake it. "I got kissed!"

"What are they like?"

They, I think. She said "they."

"They're tall and slender, like me. Black eyes. Black straight hair. A wonderful smile."

"Good-looking?"

"I don't waste my time with anybody who's toady-looking!"

We both laugh.

I run to my room and bring back the earrings. I hand her one and she holds it off to the side to put it into what eyesight she has.

"Gold." She says rubbing her thumb over it. "I can't make out the stones."

"A diamond and a ruby."

She hands it back to me. "How long have you known them?"

"A couple of weeks."

"You be careful, baby. A gift like this, so soon."

"I am careful, GeeGeema. I'm always careful."

"You just be careful-careful. Okay?"

"Yes. I will. Remember, our secret, right?"

"Right. And mine too," she says.

"Yours?"

"Just you, me, and Preston know about Stephen Wallace. Your momma? I told her that my *husband* was my first!"

*

It's cool enough after supper to bike to Eastdale. I ride the outside road and make it up the hill with no hands. After sitting on the bench, looking at the pond and woods for a while, I check for a message from Mazie. No joy. I sigh and switch off the phone. One thing about this prepay—its battery is crap.

As soon as I turn it off, it's like I'm being hugged. I think, maybe, if it wasn't for Mazie texting, I'd never carry a phone. I lean back on the bench, lift my arms, and put my hands behind my head. I wonder, like she says, if I'm showing the underside of my arms because I'm without fear or because I'm sexually submissive.

I smile. Without her, it's one thing. With her, it's both.

I watch the squirrels, not believing how much things have changed over the past two weeks, from heartbroken to...what? Love, I guess. I know I've never felt this way, that's for sure.

I try not to think too much about how I met Mazie and more about what has happened since. Rides in Fancy Car. Kisses. Gifts. But talking and being honest too. I've learned so much from her. And not just about sex. I feel my confidence growing. I know I'm braver. I don't worry so much about what people think about me. Walking around without a shirt and being a boy. Yeah, that's fun, but I know that's not the point. Being who you are is the point.

*

SK'DOO

I'm at Kazabee's side as soon as their lightning-box stops. I know I should spend my time with the Dead, but I've watched this Quick zoom from crying to smiling and I want to know why.

With some Quicks, it's confusing to connect what they do with what they think and feel. But Kazabee isn't like that. Their face is connected to their feelings. If I have any chance at all of figuring out why Quicks act the way they do, Kazabee is the place to begin.

They sigh and sit back on the bench. I think they're going to start talking to nobody like they sometimes do. Instead, they cross their legs, lift their arms in the air, and place their hands behind their head.

Their face is at rest, but I can feel the happiness. So different from crying and sad like before. I can hardly believe it's the same Quick.

As I study them, something catches my attention. I move in slowly because I know Kazabee sometimes seems to feel when I'm near.

In their ear, I see... Is that the same shiny that I-turtle found in the pond? I study it carefully. Yellow metal. White. Red.

I zoom down to Pond to look. Yellow metal. White. Red. The same! How can Pat in Pond and Kazabee have the same shiny?

I look up to see them ride down Center Road. I race to try to somehow make them see what I know, make them find the shiny, but they're intent on where they're going.

We reach Edge and there is no choice. I stop.

I go back and sit in the corner of Edge with Pat. I'll sit all night, if I need to, and all day too. I'll sit as long as I must. I'll not leave. Not even if lightning comes. I need to know what happened to Pat, and what might happen to Kazabee!

*

MAZIE

The deal was unexpectedly easy to close. They wanted him so badly that from the first sentence, it was obvious to me we'd have no trouble at all. I shake my head. The amount of money in that contract—nobody's worth that much.

It started raining this afternoon, so no golf. I'll need to get my fix some other way. No golf meant the boys headed straight to the bar. They know me well enough to not even ask.

If I want to, I'll show up, which isn't often. They don't get it, but hanging out with a bunch of drunken, alpha-male, ultra-competitive, fast-talking, know-it-all contract lawyers isn't my idea of a good time. Especially when they encroach on my personal space, which they always do, no matter how many times I warn them not to. Those types are trained to think of a no as a maybe. I suppose to make my point I could drop the worst of them to the sticky floor of a saloon with a knee to the groin. But who the hell needs the drama?

The upside to the rain is that I switched my flight, will get home at a decent hour, and be able to sleep in my own bed.

I have an hour to kill before boarding. Flying out of D.C. has one advantage: the number of international flights and their clientele guarantees upscale shops. They're small but nice.

I'm not looking to buy, but I'm dressed in something other than flip-flops and slouch-ware and so attract the attention of sales staff. I take my time and try on a couple of pieces, but nothing strikes my fancy. Besides, the prices in these places reflect the location and convenience.

As I turn to leave, something small catches my eye and makes me smile. It's perfect for Kaz. Perfect. Perfect. Perfect. I can't wait to see her face when she opens the box.

*

Bzz...

K: MAZIE!

M: Hey, KZ. How you?

K: Wonderful, now.

THANK YOU for the earrings.

They are beautiful. Like you!

M: You are perfectly welcome.

How do they look?

K: I only have one ear pierced, now,
but it looks beautiful.

M: You'll need to get the other one
redone.

I thought they'd look good against
your skin.

K: Wait...

<Image ear and jewelry KZ>

M: Nice. Even better than I thought.

K: How is D.C. and See-Sweets?

M: Finished up early. Watcha doing
tomorrow?

K: Something with you, I hope.

M: Smile. Two somethings with
me... Fun and funner.

K: New things?

M: You bet. New things.

K: YES! Can't wait.

M: See you at 1 at the bike rack.
Don't be late.

K: I'm never late when meeting MZ!

M: And no undies, cowboy or otherwise... Like me.

K: OK. No undies.

M: Good KZ. Making me happy.

I need to go to bed. I'm very tired
from the trip.

K: Wish I was there.

Night, Sleepy-MZ.

M: Night, love.

K: !!! Night. Love.

Chapter Twelve

SK'DOO

This is what I've learned after a night at Pond: Pat's life was taken by a tight hug around the neck after being given yellow metal, red, and white earrings, the shiny, by a tall, pretty Quick with dark hair and the name Mazie.

And I know Mazie! From the bench, when Kazabee first visited Dead Jimmy. I've seen them together since then.

Mazie knows Pat. Mazie gave Pat earrings. Mazie took Pat's life. Mazie must've hidden Pat in Pond when nobody, even me, would see. But Pat moved Edge. That's how I found him.

I know Kazabee doesn't know about Pat. I would feel that!

I might not know all there is to know about Quicks, but I know they do the same things over and over. Like Lady Runner, White Beard Old Man, the sextons, caretakers, and gravediggers. They all do the same things, the same way, over and over. Always.

Mazie knows Pat. Mazie gave Pat earrings. Mazie took Pat's life. Mazie put Pat in Pond.

Mazie knows Kazabee. Mazie gave Kazabee earrings... If Mazie does the same things the same way, like other Quicks, then she will take Kazabee's life and put them in Pond!

If she does, it's because of me. I made Kazabee sit on the bench. Me. I did that. Mazie came and sat. They met because of what I did.

But I don't do things that hurt!

I feel something, like lightning, only from inside. I never thought what I did mattered to Quicks. I thought I was here to listen to Deads. But I made Kazabee meet Mazie. A Quick will be Dead because of me, then be buried, and then when they say "my life is taken" I'll have to listen?

I don't do things that hurt.

I go from Pond to as close as I can get to Caretaker's without being punished by Edge and wait.

I see Kazabee, but can't tell what they're feeling because of Edge, or because I'm too far away, or both.

A machine pulls in. As it turns around, I can see a person. A Quick with black hair. Mazie.

Kazabee gets in the machine. It leaves.

Pat's a Dead. Deads never lie.

Things that happened to Pat have happened to Kazabee.

Have I hurt Kazabee?

*

KAZ

When I get in Fancy Car, the first thing I do is show Mazie the earring. She tells me I'm beautiful, pulls me to her, and kisses me on my ear, giving me a set of goose bumps that run down my right side and arm.

Then, "You need to get your other ear re-pierced."

"I'm afraid if I do, Mom'll notice and start asking questions."

"Fair point. I'll have to make do with one, I suppose." She gives me a sly look. "It would mean twice the kisses."

"Maybe I'll see if I can get it through the hole, anyway."

"That's my not-girl! But don't attract Mom's attention."

We head out from Eastdale, first south, then southwest. I see a thick, neatly folded, white blanket across the back seat. I want to ask where we're going and what we're doing, but that'd get me in trouble. She'll tell me what I need to know.

The weather is finally cooler. Some clouds with a breeze. It's a beautiful day. We're cruising along, shades on, windows down. I take off my shirt as soon as we hit the highway. Every once in a while, Mazie reaches over to pet me or demand a kiss.

We don't say much and that's okay. It's enough to be with her.

"What do you know about golf?"

"GeeGeema watches it a lot. I do with her, sometimes."

"I thought GeeGeema couldn't see."

"She can't, really, but she loves golf. She did even when she could see. It's funny, because as far as I know, she's never gone golfing. I think she knows what it's supposed to look like and sort of plugs that into what she hears."

"Weird. Do you like it?"

"I've never tried it, besides miniature golf, but it looks boring."

I get a sharp look. "Boring? You kidding me? It's the greatest game ever invented. Just you, your club, and your ball. It's all up to you. Do good? You get the credit. Screw up? It's your fault. Have you ever tried it?"

"No."

Mazie shakes her head. "You should try something before condemning it, and today you are. That's the first new thing. Are you right-handed?"

"Actually, I can use both."

"Ambidextrous?" Mazie looks at me, slyly. "Can't make up your mind about that either?"

"Not funny."

She gives me a stinging smack on the thigh with an open palm and leaves her hand there. "Lighten up, Kaz. It was a joke, not the end of the world. Which hand do you use to write?"

"Either, but I'm a little neater with my right."

"When you eat?"

"Left."

"And when you..." She slides her hand up to my crotch, squeezes, and raises her eyebrows.

I feel those muscles twitch and wish I didn't blush so much. "Whichever feels best."

"A switch hitter—how lucky you are!" She moves her hand back to the wheel. "I'm a lefty"—she grins—"no matter the activity. We'll get you a right-hand club, just in case."

"We're going golfing?"

"With you?" She laughs. "Hell, no! Nine would take all day, even shooting short-hole. We'll hit a couple buckets so you start to get a feel for it."

"Buckets?"

"You'll see. Put your shirt on, we're here."

"Country Driving Range," the sign says. It looks sort of run-down, and it's not very busy.

She pops the trunk and starts to pull a couple of clubs from the bag there. She stops, giving me some money. "Make yourself useful. Get two big buckets, tell the guy how tall you are, and ask for a right-hand seven-iron. Meet me at the far end of the tees to the left. You'll see me there."

"Right-hand seven-iron. Tees to the left. Should I get you a bottle of water too?"

She glances at me. "If I wanted one, I'd ask."

I do as I'm told, sort of struggling to carry everything. Like the beach, I think. It's part of being with her. There's a line of patches of very fake grass with small rubber tubes sticking up out of them.

"You're at the very end," she directs. Mazie leans all three clubs against the parking lot fence behind us and has me place a bucket of golf balls on the patches we'll be using. She takes a neon-orange glove from her back pocket and starts pulling it on.

"What's that for?"

"To make my tan look great."

"Okaaay... There's some change."

"Keep it." She picks a golf ball out of a bucket and tosses

it at me. "Hey, Kaz! Think fast."

I manage to catch it.

"Right hand," she says, picking up the club I got at the counter. "Crap iron. But good enough. What do you know about golf?"

"I know that you hold the straight end of the club, use the bent end to hit a ball, and hope it goes where you want."

I feel wonderful when she laughs. "I've never heard a better description of the game. But you lack detail. Let me show you what you're trying for, so you can have a goal."

She puts a ball on one of the tubes, tees, in front of her. Swings her arms up over her head, pauses, then swings down and hits the ball, smooth and effortless.

"It didn't go very far."

She raises her right eyebrow and glares over her sunglasses. "My beautiful and technically perfect swing and that's all you have to say? 'It didn't go very far.'" She sighs and shakes her head. "I should make you wait in the car. I should make you wait in the car's trunk! Look up the row behind me. Every person who's trying to hit the ball as far as they can is an idiot. For every long shot, there are two or three where the most important thing is being able to put the ball where it needs to be."

She looks out into the range. "Watch that 150 sign." Mazie hits another ball. It sails through the air and bangs off the sign.

"Wow."

"Damned right 'wow.' I'm even better when I bother to wear the correct shoes. Now, let's start with the grip."

My first swing, I hit the fake grass with a loud enough thump that some of the other people look at me and grin.

"Don't blush!" she growls. "Every single one of these idiots, no matter how good they are, started the same exact way as you are, right now. Don't pay any attention to them. It's you, the club, and the ball. Understand?"

I nod, then take a few more swings and manage to actually hit the ball a few feet. It doesn't fly through the air but bounces along the ground.

"You're trying too hard. Leading with your arms. Here." She stands behind me, hooks the fingers of one hand through my center belt loop, and grabs the hair on the back of my head with the other.

"Look at the ball." She tilts my head. "The ball! Feet wider apart. Good. Point them forward. Bend your knees a little. Keep them parallel, you're not cowboying a horse, or a man!"

"Not cowboying," I repeat.

She tries to move my hips. "What are you, a statue? Let your knees move. And your waist. Good. I'm going to hold your head still and move your hips in the direction we want the ball to go."

She sways my bottom half back and forth. "Feel what that's like? Swing your arms up so your club is level with the ground. Keep that leading arm straight. I'm going to move your hips. Look at the ball! When your shoulders start to tilt, with that arm straight, drop the club in an arc. Nice, easy, and without power. Ready?"

"Without power. Okay."

I manage to hit the ball. With a nice click against the club, it flies to land several feet away!

"Nice shot!" She hugs me from behind and kisses the side of my neck. We do a couple more with the same reward for each. Then she lets me try on my own.

The shot doesn't go as far, but it goes.

She steps up and kisses me on the mouth. "Good job!"

"Thanks." I smile.

She hugs me, lowering her voice to a near whisper. "Right now. Right this instant. Are you female, nonbinary, or male?"

"I'm not thinking about that. I'm just happy."

She steps back, tilts her head, and smiles. "See how that works? Now, where that last one landed? See how close you can hit the rest of them."

I take my time, taking bigger and bigger swings and learning all about whiffs, chunks, fats, and duffs as I go. I slowly improve to the point that I sort of know where the ball might end up.

Every one of her shots is beautiful. She hits near and far, high and low, all with the same club.

"Where'd you learn to golf so good?"

Mazie shrugs. "C-Suites and lawyers love golf. More deals are made on the course than in the office. They bet on golf too."

"You win lots of money?"

"No. Bad for business. Unless there's an idiot who needs to be put back in his place." Her eyes sparkle as she shows her teeth. "In that case, I crush him in front of his male associates. Under those circumstances, having a girl beat your best game by ten strokes is even more humiliating."

After the second bucket, she declares we're done. "Take the empties and your club back to the counter. Get a couple bottles of water while you're there. I'll meet you at the car." She picks up her gear and walks off.

As I buy the water, the guy at the little building gives me a gap-toothed grin. "Buddy, I got no idea what you're payin' for them kinda of lessons—whatever it is"—he winks—"it's worth it!"

Mazie and I are back in Fancy Car, sunglasses off, each with a bottle of water, windows up and air conditioner running.

"A guy called me 'buddy.' That never happened before!"

"Like the beach. If you present anything close to a teenage boy, and a very beautiful woman is kissing you, then you're a 'buddy.' There's nothing else you could be." She taps the side of her head. "Cars speeding by, remember? Idiots are always sure of what you are, even though you're not. You getting it yet?"

"Yeah. I think I'm starting to. How did I do at golf?"

"You mean at that one single very small part of the game? Acceptable, for a beginner. Likely to improve with practice."

I smile. "Good." I point at the palm of my hand. "Look, I almost got a blister."

She smiles back. "You know that orange glove? Besides making my tan look great, it also keeps that from happening."

"*Now* you tell me."

Another smile. She points to the dash. "Look, there."

I open it. Inside is a small, red box. "Mazie. Not more jewelry! I haven't given you anything."

"You have no idea what you've given me. Open it."

There's red tissue inside. Between the layers is a small silver object. I hold it in my right palm and look at her, confused. "You got me a baby fish?"

Mazie laughs louder than I've ever heard. "No, dummy.

It's a tadpole."

"Tadpole?"

"Yes. A tadpole. A polliwog." She looks at me, eyebrows together, head tilted. "You *do* know what a tadpole is, don't you?"

"Yeah. It's a baby frog. So, you got me a baby frog?"

She sighs. "It's not a 'baby frog,' Kaz. A tadpole is a transitional form between egg and adult. It's not what it started out as, and it's not what it'll end up being. It doesn't know what it is yet. It's stuck for a while. Like you." Mazie smiles, her eyes so gentle.

Mine fill with tears. I nod at her. "Like me. For a while."

"Do you like it?"

"I love it." I hug her. "I'll keep it forever."

"Kiss me."

Her lips are cold and wet from the water.

Her face serious, she runs a hand down over my jeans, hooks her fingers under my crotch, and tugs. "Golf was one new thing. Let's move on to the next, my pretty perfect polliwog."

*

MAZIE

I head back toward town. The pitching lesson was a little bit of fun. A way to lower defenses. She appreciated my gift as I knew she would, endearing me to her even more. The look on her face, when she understood its significance, was wonderful.

Now, let's test some limits. About halfway back, there's a turn from the main road. I can tell she wants to ask where we're going, but she won't.

"Mill Valley State Park." I smile at her. "Been here?"

"No." Soft, wide, brown eyes.

"Wait until you see. It's gorgeous." And beautifully deserted. Nobody ever comes to these parks. The state is wasting a ton of my tax dollars on upkeep.

The parking lot is empty. I use the spot closest to the trail I want to take. When we get out of the car, I walk to her, put my right hand around her waist, and pull her tight, moving my hips slightly against hers. I don't know if she realizes what she's doing, but she responds in kind. I kiss her mouth, then bite her neck, not to leave a mark, but hard enough to let her know I mean business.

Kaz melts into my arms and leans against me.

I shake her off. "Get the blanket in the back. I want to show you something. It's not very far. I like it. So will you."

I take off and she hurries to catch up. As we walk side-by-side, I stick my hand down the back of her jeans. With each step, I feel her glutes work. Nice, thin, tight.

"There was an old mill here," I say. "Gone now. We're going to part of the property it sat upon."

What remains of the mill is down in the valley, along the stream. But that's too distant. If what I have in mind works, I don't want the trip back to be too far.

"Here we are."

"Mazie, it's beautiful."

And it is. We've walked around the end of a high dry-stone wall to look out over an open valley and can see down to the mill stream and a little bit beyond to a far row of trees.

I take the blanket. "Why aren't you helping me with this?"

We unfold it, take two corners, and tuck them between the stones in the wall about three feet up. The rest covers the ground.

I sit on it, lean back against the wall, spread my legs, and pat the blanket between them. She kneels, facing me, unsure of what to do. I love that look. I give a kiss, take her by her slim shoulders, and turn her to face the valley. "Here. Sit."

When she does, I hook my fingers in the belt loops of her jeans and pull so she scoots back to me. I place my feet between her knees and spread her legs to match mine. My fingers tingle. It feels so good to have her close and in her place. I inhale. Her skin and hair smell wonderful. I look at her profile. Kaz is a beauty with not a thing wrong with her. Smart. Quick to learn. Given time, she'd only improve, of that I'm certain.

She leans up against me, snuggles, and sighs. "This is so nice. I wish we could stay like this forever."

Almost breathless, I lift the front of my shirt and back of hers so our naked skin touches. Putting my arms around her waist, I give a little squeeze and pull her tight against me. She fits, just right, like none of the others have. I nuzzle the top of her shoulder through her shirt. Goose bumps run down her arms and her pulse quickens even more in the side of her lovely, lovely neck.

I whisper in her sweet left ear. "Do you remember, at the beach, what I told you?

She shivers. Eyes crinkle in thought. "The beach?"

Popping the plosives, barely pronouncing the vowels, stressing the consonants I speak on the inhale and exhale, so softly my voice is barely there. "Yes, about testing reality? I said I could sit behind you, hold you so you couldn't move, stick my tongue in your ear, bite your neck, jam my hand down your crotch, and rub you from one orgasm to the next, and the world still wouldn't end."

She shies away a bit. I pull her back in against me.

I slide my hands under her tee and run them over that smooth, soft, cool skin. I feel delicious tiny tremors running through her, and me. My voice is unsteady. "What did you say about that?"

She surrenders, chin up, throat exposed, the side of her head against mine. "That we should make sure that was true."

"That's exactly what we're going to do, my Lovely-Sweet-Kaz. Are you afraid somebody might see us?"

Her eyes are closed. Her breathless speech is quietly slurred, as if she's drugged. "No, Mazie. I'm brave. Like you."

Oh, the possibilities granted by that statement. I slide my hands down her torso. She sucks in her tummy. I touch her right hand. "Unfasten your jeans."

Kaz unbuttons and unzips them, moving to take them off.

"No," I whisper. "All we need is a little bit of room."

I put my shaking right arm across her chest, resting that hand on her left shoulder and holding her close. I slide my left hand down the front of her jeans.

"Now you know why no undies."

"Yes," she repeats, quietly. "Now I know."

She's soaking wet and I'm moving in that same direction. This isn't going to take long. I lead her right to the brink, then stop, take her left hand, and push it in that direction.

She resists. "I can't."

"Yes," I whisper in her ear and give her hand a slight tap.

She takes over.

I slowly move my left hand to behind her head and place my right hand in the crook of my left elbow. A perfect choke with a perfect name: rear naked.

I wish there was an earring on this side, but I suppose the world can't always be perfect.

I wait for only a few moments.

Her breath quickens. Free hand comes up behind her head. Legs try to straighten, but I use my feet to keep her knees parted. I'm sure, were her shoes off, I'd see her toes curl. A blush on her throat. Pulse races. She twists her neck to see my face. Pupils dilated. Her eyes roll back. "Oh, Mazie..." She bucks, then arches. Muscles in her neck stand free. Breathes in and holds it. Holds it. Holds it. A slight sound, deep in her throat. Over she goes.

I push myself against her. Tighten my arms. Over I go too.

*

SK'DOO

I've spent all day in the woods, not listening to the Dead, but watching Pond and thinking about Kazabee being there.

I don't know what to do. What *can* I do? I am almost nothing to Quicks! What can an almost-nothing do about anything?

I've decided that if Mazie is putting Kazabee in Pond, she'll do it at night. Too many Quicks can see during the day.

I'll keep watching. I can't do anything else.

*

KAZ

I blink.

From far away. "Kaz! Kaz!"

Things come back into focus, slowly, from a gray center out. Blue sky. Clouds. My ears are ringing.

"Kaz!" A hard slap on my face. Worried, shining black eyes.

"Mazie. What happened?"

Hand to forehead, she sits. Her face is flushed. "You're okay."

"What happened?"

"What do you remember?"

"I was sitting against you. You were holding and kissing me. You and I... I started... Did I faint?"

"You scared the hell out of me, going limp in my arms

like that. I thought you were dead!"

"I'm sorry. I get dizzy sometimes, but I never fainted before. How long was I out?"

"A couple of minutes, at least. Once I saw you were breathing, I thought maybe you were having a seizure. Can you walk?"

"Don't know. Give me a little time." She helps me sit. I lean back against the wall. "I have kind of a headache. Why is the front of my shirt wet?"

"You drooled."

"Eww. Ick. Great." I look at Mazie. "Now I'm fainting. Something else for me to worry about."

She reaches out and touches the earring I'm wearing. "Maybe you need to wear fall-protection gear. You'll look extra-cute in a safety harness."

I laugh. Then start to cry. We sit on the blanket, her holding me until I'm done with both.

I have a little trouble getting back to the car. I can tell Mazie's worried because she carries the blanket. But by the time we finish the drive back to Eastdale, I feel fine. She wants to follow me the rest of the way. I tell her I'll be okay and promise to text her as soon as I get home.

Once there, I tell GeeGeema I'm going to take a nap and climb onto my bed. I send the text I promised, then check the Internet.

There it is. Fainting during intense orgasms. It's a thing. Great.

*

MAZIE

Christ, that was a close call. Stupid and careless of me to even consider playing around like that. It took every ounce of resolve to release my hold. Even then, she was out for so long that I thought she might not recover. Scared the living hell out of me.

There I'd be with a body, and no way to dispose of it.

Stupid. Stupid. Stupid.

It's dumb luck she made it. That's all there is to it. And luck is nothing to base my activities on. Being caught in some errant sex act is one thing. Being caught with the departed...

As much as I hate to admit it, today taught me that I can't trust myself with her. I'm out of my depth. Beyond my expertise. I probably would've never started were it not for the leverage provided by her stupid gender crap. Had I listened to myself, I wouldn't have suffered today's scare. I know that much.

If I'm absolutely honest with myself, I'll admit I'm attracted to her. And that very notion is clouding my judgment.

She's a *toy*. I remind myself. Nothing more.

I breathe to regain my calm. No self-incrimination. That doesn't help. Never has. Never will. I need to decide how to complete this project and stick to that decision.

Adding her to my list would be wonderful. I smile. Drain her sparkling life. Make it disappear. I tingle at the thought. She'd finally have decent clothes, a great haircut, appropriate makeup, and polish on her long pretty fingers and toes, earrings in both ears, as is proper. She'd be gorgeous.

No. Out of the question. This is far more complicated than a shiny present then the end of all things. Too much time for her to tell or hint about me—perhaps to Bouncing Red at work, or GeeGeema, if no one else. I've no killing site nor anything remotely similar to a disposal plan. How do I move someone who is my weight? Dismemberment? Never!

Besides, we are tied by the death of Chunky Dude. And plenty of witnesses have seen us together. Cops are dumb, but not *that* dumb. In order to continue as safely as I was before this debacle, it is imperative I never become a "person of interest," for any reason.

Maybe I can force a decision she'll regret. Figure out what she wants to be and convince her to be something else. That would damage her, for sure. But to do that, I need a relationship with her, and that's too dangerous because, sooner or later, she would reveal me to others. Or she'd slide from toy to target, or worse, toy to lover. Then I'd be stuck right where I am now.

I entered this enterprise with the intent to play and leave. Scope creep is a sign of poor management in any project. It's time to move on.

Kaz is so in love with me. Establishing that emotion was ridiculously simple. All I had to do was make her feel cherished for her own confused self.

So, I'll back off immediately. It will be easy to convince her the breakup is all her fault. That I've decided I can't stand being with her. I'll tie it to her dysphoria, tell her I need a real woman or man, not some silly child too weak and confused to make up their mind. Who could love a freak who dithers ineffectually between the two? I'll include the fainting; tell her it frightens me so badly that she's made me incapable of intimacy.

Then I'll watch her struggle. It should be interesting to see how that affects me. A minor twinge of guilt can be instructive. Especially since I've not felt any for a long time.

At the very least, the cutting will restart and leave permanent reminders of her stupidity and weakness. As wonky as her psyche is, she might kill herself.

Unlike Chunky Dude and the accident, and attracted to

her, or not, I'd gladly add Dead-Kaz to my list, as long as I'm sure I can take credit. Her death would destroy her family, her precious GeeGeema, especially.

Maybe I could sneak in during the funeral's visiting hours and critique the undertaker's work which would be, without a doubt, inferior to my own. I've never seen the results of my efforts displayed in that manner. All those people, looking at what I've accomplished. What a thrill that would be.

As a bonus, she'd likely be buried in that run-down wreck of a cemetery. I'd have three beauties to visit—all in one place. Who could ask for anything more?

One way or the other, I'll be free of her in less than a week.

*

Bzz...

> *M:* You feeling better?

>> *K:* Yeah. I'm resting in bed a little.
>> Kind of scary.

> *M:* Don't worry, there's an explanation.

>> *K:* I'm not going to a doctor until it

happens more than once.

I spoiled everything.

M: Yes. You did.

K: I'm so sorry... It was scary.

What you were doing before it happened felt really good.

Maybe, next time... We'll see if YOU faint!

May I see you tomorrow?

M: You work?

K: No. Another day off.

M: Me too. Let's meet at 10:30.

K: OK. Thanks for the golf lessons!

M: You are welcome.

K: We can do that anytime. Golf is harder than it looks.

M: Yes. Like many things.

K: Goodnight, MZ. Love you.

M: 'Night.

*

KAZ

I'm getting ready for bed, putting on my moisturizer after a day in the sun. Standing in front of the mirror, I'm thinking I don't look too bad. Collarbones, flat chest, ribs, hips, boy-butt, and all the rest. Not skinny—slender. Mazie thinks I'm beautiful. And if she thinks I'm beautiful, that's good enough for me.

I stand straighter, that's for sure. No slouching! It's good to be tall. I'm braver too. I've done so many things over the last couple of weeks that I never thought of doing. So much fun. So bad too. I watch myself blush a little, but it doesn't bother me. After so long, I'm finally okay being who I am: just Kaz.

It'll be wonderful to see her tomorrow. I try so hard to make her happy. I love her. Like GeeGeema loves Stephen Wallace.

I look closely at my face. It's not stupid-looking any-more. I smile at myself. Automatic no gums. I smile wider, then that fades. It's a shame Jimmy had to die to bring Mazie and me together. If I had to choose between the two...but it's more than that. It would be Jimmy and old me or new me and Mazie. I shake my head. That's something I can't control. There's no use even going there.

Something catches my eye. On the left side of my neck. I twist my head to the right but can't quite see. I pick up my hand mirror, hold it so I use its reflection. I lean close.

I look, blink, look again. My eyebrows knit. I stare into my own eyes for what seems like a long time.

There's one thing I'm suddenly sure of. It's time for everyone to be honest.

Chapter Thirteen

KAZ

I put Preston's food on the floor, give him a careful pet on his head, and take a cup of water to GeeGeema.

I sit in the chair across from her.

"GeeGeema, do you believe in always telling the truth?"

"Child, you ask such hard questions these days. Don't you want to know why the sky is blue or how clouds float?"

I laugh. "Life gets more complicated as you go, I guess."

"And then it gets simpler again." She pauses. "Always being honest is a hard thing. You can't always tell the truth, like when a friend gets an ugly hairdo. Sometimes you got to encourage them to the truth."

"Encourage?"

"Steer them away from that bad haircut. Sometimes, though, you gotta kick somebody in the behind with the truth. Get them back on the straight and narrow!"

"How about important things?"

"You remember back when you were feeling so sad."

"Yes."

"How I told you that I loved you no matter what?"

"I remember."

"I told you the truth because it was important. Important for you to hear and for me to say. Telling the truth makes it real in your heart. Your old brain might think it. But until you say it, it's just an idea. Once you say it, it becomes something: the truth. And that's what you can put in your heart."

"But what if you're afraid to tell the truth?"

"That's the most important time to say it. So many times, being afraid is your brain and your heart not knowing what the other is doing. Your brain isn't so good at things, and your heart isn't so good at ideas. It's telling the truth that ties them together."

I look at that face so old. "I love you no matter what."

"I already know that, Kaz, but it's always nice to hear."

"Thanks." I give her a hug, stand, and straighten my

back.

"You off to tell the truth?"

"Yes. I am off to tell the truth!"

*

SK'DOO

I watched Pond all night. No Kazabee. I go to Hill, where I can see everything.

"Momma says little things get big things done."

"Thank you, Ezme."

I see Kazabee by Caretaker's. Kazabee.

As I move toward them, the dark machine comes in and stops.

*

MAZIE

She's holding flowers in her hand. For me? How sweet. I lower the window on her side of the vehicle. "Get in."

"Please, Mazie. It's such a beautiful day, please. Let's just walk and talk. Okay? Please?" She holds out her hand.

I give her a stern look, then pretend to relent. "Walk? Better not be far." As I get out of the car, she fairly skips to me and gives me a kiss which I don't return.

"Still with just one earring?" I grouse. "Why did I even bother buying you two?"

Annoyingly, her mood doesn't dim. "You like?" She holds three red rosebuds. Then makes a face and shifts them around in her hands. "Ow! They have thorns, y'know."

"They're roses, what do you expect? Where'd you get them?"

"An old guy down the street from me. Mr. Mazza. He grows them along his house. He was out this morning, and I stopped and asked if I could have some."

"You asked an old guy for flowers out of his garden?"

She laughs. "I'm brave, remember? Besides, he only had a thousand of them so I went up to him and asked. It was like you said on the beach, about being in charge and trading back and forth. It was easy!"

My eyebrows lift. Who is this person standing in front of me?

She holds out her right hand. "C'mon, let's walk."

*

SK'DOO

As soon as they're on my side of Edge I follow as closely as I can, kept away by the lightning-box in Mazie's back pocket. I know that holding hands is something Quicks do when they're friends, but I don't feel that from both.

To Pond, I think as hard as I can. *Kazabee go to Pond!*

*

MAZIE

I let her lead, for a change. If anything, I'm curious as to how all of this is going to turn out. We walk along the center gravel road. I'm sure the flowers are for Chunky Dude. I hide my smirk as we start up the rise and she, so predictably, veers off to the left. We pace to the grave of her friend. The one I killed.

"I hope this grass isn't too wet."

"Please don't be like that, Mazie."

She places a single flower on the now partially sunken mound of earth. At first, I think I'm going to suffer through some sort of prayer. She turns and gives me a short fierce hug instead.

"We met on that bench." She looks in that direction, then into my eyes. "It was the day Jimmy was buried. I know you didn't kill him. He died because of a mistake, not because of anything we did." She sighs. "It doesn't make sense. It probably never will. I miss him so much and wish he was still alive, and I'm sad he's not. At the same time, the only reason I met you is because he died. Mazie, I'm so happy we know each other, but sometimes I feel bad about it. It's confusing."

Again, with a strong hug, which like the other, and the kiss, I do not return.

"And the other flowers?"

She takes my hand and smiles. "You'll see."

Up the hill we go. She leads me to the pond side of the bench.

I balk and pull my hand away. "Kaz. No!"

*

SK'DOO

Finally here! Finally. And without my steering. It would be better without Mazie, but there will be no other chance. Before they stop walking, I back up, and ignoring the zings from Mazie's lightning-box, I zoom to slam into Kazabee. I bump against their feet, steering them to where they need to be.

*

KAZ

As I reach the far side of the bench, I grow dizzy and stumble. The only way I can keep my balance is by grabbing

Mazie's arm.

*

MAZIE

The damned klutz suddenly grabs my wrist and stumbles down the embankment. Pulled along, I nearly fall on my face.

"Hey!" I jerk my arm from her grasp. "Cut it the hell out!"

"I'm sorry, I didn't mean to." She recovers, looking at the pond then me with pleading eyes. "I know she's important to you, Mazie. I could tell from what you told me in the car, by the way you talked about her. Her ashes were scattered here in the water. She's somebody you love. Right?"

"Kaz..." I warn.

She reaches with her left hand to push my hair behind my right ear. "I know there were people before me. I know you've loved others. You're so smart and so beautiful. You could love anybody you wanted, and they would love you back. Like I do."

I move away from her touch. "You're being ridiculous."

She ignores my tone. "I know you love her because you visit her all the time. I understand if you don't want to tell me. But she has no marker. Only you and I know she's here. She wants to be forgotten. But I know you can't forget her, can you?" Her eyes fill with tears.

A little too close to home, that one. I swallow.

"Mazie. Please. It'll help you feel better. I promise."

I'm thinking that, were we in the car, I'd slap her for her persistence. Instead, I glare, grind my teeth, and remain silent. Anything to shut her the hell up.

Kaz tosses a flower onto the water.

There's a momentary silence.

Still holding the third rose, she looks at me, face blank. "I know you choked me."

I step away. "What?"

"At the wall. Yesterday." She says evenly. "I didn't faint. You choked me."

"Kaz, I don't know..."

She cuts me off with a look. "Friends don't lie, remember?" Keeping her eyes on mine, she turns her head to the right and points to the muscles on the left side of her throat. "Look."

I lean in. "I don't see..."

"Look close. Real close."

There, against her smooth skin, faintly visible, is a bruise.

"You could've got that from anything," I start.

"You're lying, Mazie. Look again. You can *see* the truth."

I comply and find she's right: I can see the truth. The pattern of the bruise matches the Greek box chain around my right wrist.

I struggle to recover. "Kaz. It's not what you think."

She smiles. "I know what it is. All last night I thought about what happened at the wall. When we started, you had your right arm across my chest holding me against you. You were using your left hand on me. When you had me take over, you put your left hand behind my head."

I have nothing to say.

"It was easy to look up. Rear naked choke." Not a question. A statement of fact.

Dumbfounded. Caught. I'm caught. A child caught me.

"The way you did it? Right-handed. So, now you know you're not a lefty for *everything*." Her eyes shine as she widens her smile. "And I figured out why you choked me too."

I'm alarmed. "You did?"

Kaz nods and smiles slyly. "Erotic asphyxiation. Right? I looked that up too. People getting off by choking someone or from being choked. That's why your face was flushed when I came to from you choking me. You came too, from you choking me!" She grins at her play on words. "I think it's why you always touch me around my neck and throat. You think it's hot to choke people."

Smart, I remind myself. Too damned smart. I feign embarrassment, looking at the ground and scratching the back of my head. "I don't know what to say."

She grabs the hair on the back of my head and kisses me, hard. She touches my lips with the tip of her tongue as she disengages. A shiver runs down my spine. When I breathe out, it's shaky.

"Don't blush!" Shyly. "We'll try again, but you have to let me go further, y'know, so I get more out of it."

"Further? More out of it?"

"Yeah. You knocked me out before I had any real fun. Maybe next time, don't squeeze as hard and sort of put me out just a little instead of all the way. Y'know, see what that's like?" She sparkles. "I'll still wear the safety harness, if you want me to." Then, she looks at me sternly. "But you have to give me some warning when you're gonna do something new like that. Just a clue. Don't tell me everything. I like surprises. And I trust you—you'd never hurt me. You know a lot more about a lot of things, especially sex, and you might be worried that I'm not into what you want to do, but please don't do something new and then try to hide it, okay? I mean, don't lie. I don't like liars. And it makes you kind of like those idiots you talked about at the beach, the ones who think they don't have to trade power and try to take what they want. That's not you," she says seriously, shaking her head. "You'd never want to be an idiot. Would you?"

"No, I wouldn't."

She steps to me, wraps her arms around my waist, pulls herself in tight, and leans back so our hipbones mesh.

"I know you're sort of grumpy, sometimes. And you hate it when I slouch or ask too many questions. And I know I'm supposed to tell you everything even though you keep secrets." She kisses me on the cheek. "But none of that matters, because I want to be with you so much it makes my bones ache!"

Well, shit. This new dynamic blows me completely out of the water. It's not control when the other person gives you permission, is it? Me, big-shot negotiator. Best in the business. Outsmarted by a gender-dysphoric, puberty-halted, maybe-not-a-female teenager. No. I wasn't outsmarted. I was clueless. From the get-go.

I start to laugh.

Her brows knit. "What's so funny?"

I look into her beautiful, shining, brown eyes. For a long moment, with her holding me, we are alone in the world. I smile and run my fingers through her loose curls. "I was thinking, my dear, sweet polliwog, about how one person can change the other."

Glowing with emotion, Kaz lets go, steps back, then astonishes me with a deep curtsy. She holds out the last flower. "I saved this one for you."

When I take it from her hand a thorn jabs me. "Ouch! Dammit!" I drop the bud and put my thumb in my mouth.

"I'll get it!" she chirps.

When she stands back up, she's not holding the rose. There on her open left palm is a simple gold hoop earring with a diamond and ruby, one above the other. A piece of earlobe still attached.

I stand, stunned. How the hell... *I should've sewn the cloth shut!* I involuntarily look at the pond's spillway. When I look back at Kaz, I realize my mouth is open. When I shut it, my teeth click.

With a confused look on her face, she reaches up and touches her right ear. "Mazie..." Her voice is a whisper. "What did you do?"

I backpedal.

Confusion to comprehension to horror. "My God, Mazie. What did you *do*?"

In that instant, my perfectly ordered existence unspools. All my planning. All my prep. All my care. All I've done. All my life. All of it. All. Of. It. Undone. Rendered meaningless by this confused piece of genderless trash tossing *fucking* flowers into a *fucking* pond. I should've stuck with what I was best at. I was an idiot to think she was worth my attention!

"Kaz..." I step, then grab her wrist. She leans back, takes my arm, twists, and bends it to an awkward angle. I feel a crunch and instant pain. I misstep and fall backwards. There's a snapping sound from my back pocket. Yet another broken phone.

"You idiot bitch. I am so gonna *kill* your skinny brown ass." Consumed by fury, I regain my feet and turn to take her down. I know I can end her, despite my newly broken arm. She attacked me first. I'll claim self-defense. I surrender to an overwhelming cold rage. Who cares what I claim? I don't give a goddam what happens to me as long as this piece of shit is dead!

As I reach her, I am frozen in place. Sounds. Loud voices. Flashing colors like bright police lights but a thousand times worse. Growing agony in my eyes. My head. I speak. It's not me. Not my words. Not my voice. Confused, I twirl. Scream. Stumble. Knees. Feet. Stand. Flee. *Run!* There's a flash.

*

KAZ

Mazie jabs herself with a thorn. "Ouch! Dammit!" She drops the bud and puts her thumb in her mouth like she's a little kid.

I smile at the idea of her being small, in cutoffs and bare feet. "I'll get it!"

When I reach down to pick up the rose, just in the corner of my eye, maybe, there's a glimmer. Right on the edge of the water. My fingers tingle and move as if on their own to pick it up. There's a moment before I realize what it is... An earring, like mine, with mud on it. I stand with it in my left hand. As I do, I realize that what I think is mud is dirty flesh.

Mazie's looking at the far side of the pond, at the spillway. When she turns back to me, her mouth is open. When she shuts it, her teeth click.

I reach up and touch the matching earring I'm wearing. "Mazie..." I say softly. "What did you do?"

She backs away from me.

I realize that if I'm holding jewelry with a piece of an ear, there's a whole lot more. "My God, Mazie... What did you *do*?"

She stares at me, eyes wide, the color rising in her face. Her brows come together. She changes; sharp, danger, poison.

"Kaz..." she warns as she grabs me by the wrist. I take her arm like GeeGeema taught me, twist it, bend it. There's a snap.

She stumbles and falls on her butt. She crouches. "You

idiot bitch," she growls in a low, deep voice, "I am so gonna *kill* your skinny brown ass."

Her beautiful, terrifying, purple rage pins me in my place. She stands, moves to me, then suddenly bends at the waist. Shaking her head. Running her hands over a pain-twisted face.

"Kazabee!" Mazie yells in a voice I've never heard. She spins, howls like an animal, falls, thrashes, gets up, and runs for the woods.

There's a bright flash. Like bouncing off an invisible wall, she staggers and falls into the pond face-first.

*

SK'DOO

See it, Kazabee! Pick it up. I think as hard as I can. Through the pain from Mazie's lightning-box, I steer Kazabee's fingers to it, right next to Pond. I back away.

It's held out. "Mazie... What did you do?"

Kazabee tries to reject, then suddenly understands and accepts the truth about Mazie, Pat, and Pond.

"My God, Mazie. What did you *do*?"

They struggle. Mazie falls. Her lightning-box stops working.

"You idiot bitch. I am so going to *kill* your skinny brown

ass."

To keep Kazabee safe, I fly to push myself into Mazie's head. It hurts. More than machinery. More than lightning-boxes. More than Edge. More even than lightning itself!

Mazie falls, shouts, stands, and runs. Runs straight into Edge.

There's a flash.

*

KAZ

"Mazie!" I run to her, grab her legs, and pull her from the pond. "Mazie! Please, please, please!" I roll her over, wet, black, straight hair plastered across her forehead. Eyes open. Blood and gore on her beautiful face. A wide-open crack in the right side of her head where she hit the edge of the dam.

I see her brains, and puke into the water.

"Excuse me," comes a voice from up on the hill.

Wiping my mouth on my sleeve, I turn and look.

The old man with the white beard is standing near the bench. "Do you need help?"

"Yes! Please! Get somebody."

He turns to hurry down the gravel road.

"Oh, Mazie." I put my head on her chest and start to cry.

*

I talk to the same police officers I did when Jimmy was killed. The ambulance takes me to the hospital where I'm treated for shock.

Chapter Fourteen

KAZ

I don't remember anything about the rest of day Mazie died, including my parents bringing me home. The whole next day is a blur too. I think they drugged me.

I wish I had more of whatever they used.

The day after that, mid-morning, a big, dark SUV with government plates pulls in. The driver gets out, and before anybody in the house has time to panic, I walk out to meet them.

"Ms. Delcorio?" I'm shown a badge and ID. "I'm Marcella Echelle with the Federal Government. Do you have time to talk?"

"Am I in trouble?"

"You've committed no crime. Please. It would help us a great deal if you could spare a few minutes."

I hesitate. "Do I have to?"

"No, but please," she repeats. "It would help us if you did."

"Okay, I guess. You want to come in the house?"

She tilts her head toward the vehicle. "Maybe, for this first time, privacy would be best."

I run to the front door and yell that everything is fine and I'm not going anywhere, then walk to the car. She opens the back door on the passenger's side. I climb in; she gets in behind me and shuts the door. I slide all the way over to the far side and check. There are handles.

She motions to the front seat. "This is Albertson Williamson."

"Albertson Williamson the Third, if you please," he replies in a very deep voice. "Yeah. I'm Al."

She has clear blue eyes and a broad smile. Athletic with a sort of a hawkish look. Seems very neat and organized. Short brown hair, seriously going gray. He's older and sort of scruffy with rimless glasses and a poorly trimmed silver beard. What hair he has is bed-headed, and he looks like he sleeps in his clothes.

"Ms. Delcorio…" she asks, "okay if we use first names?"

I shrug.

"Please call me Marcy," she says as she takes a small device, turns it on, and places it on the seat between us. "I'll be recording this. Do you understand?"

I nod.

"I'm sorry, but you have to speak your answer."

"Fine. I understand. I'm being recorded."

"Thanks." She announces the time, date, location, topic, and who's in the car, then looks at me. "You've had a couple of rough days, Kaz. You doing okay?"

"I'm dealing."

"I'm afraid my partner and I are going to make things a whole lot tougher for you. Let me know if it gets to be too much, okay?"

My stomach does a flip-flop, but I nod. "Yeah. Okay."

She looks at her partner. "Al, the folder?"

"Yeah. Sure." He passed her a thick envelope. "Here y'are."

She pulls out several stapled sheets of paper and hands them to me. "Ever see this before?"

A color copy. Sets of numbers. Each followed by lines of neatly written letters and symbols. I shake my head.

"Please speak your answer."

"No. I've never seen them before. Are they Mazie's?"

"From her home. Mean anything to you?"

"No. But I know she liked puzzles. She said she did crosswords and triple acrostic poetry, whatever that is, in ink, using German and...French, I think."

"That's really good to know." She takes the pages back and writes a note on the top of the first one. "We haven't figured it out, but we will. It's a list, obviously. GPS coordinates and descriptions we think. Of what, we can't say exactly, but it's pretty easy to guess."

She hands me more pages. Each holds pictures of the faces of very pretty, sleeping kids. "We found these too. Very well hidden. Twenty-three. Same as the number of entries on the list."

"Those we came very close to *not* finding," the guy says, lifting his shaggy eyebrows. "They weren't filed 'M' for murder."

I feel myself getting light-headed. "They're not sleeping? They're dead?"

Marcy taps one of the images. "This one was in the pond. But there's something else." She points to an ear of one of the kids. "Take a closer look. All of them have these."

I lean in. A simple gold hoop earring with a diamond and ruby, one above the other.

I grimace as my stomach turns. I swallow hard, tasting bile.

Al clears his throat. "Look, Kaz, if you feel the need to barf, do it out the door, okay?"

"Mazie killed kids?"

"Yeah," he says gently, nodding slightly. "Lots of kids."

"Mazie killed kids," I repeat. "Mazie killed kids." As if saying it will help me understand. We sit, silent, for several moments.

"What the hell makes you kill kids?"

"Hard to tell at this point," Marcy says. "Typically, it's about power and control. For some, it's acting out against their own childhood experiences of abuse by others. There's also the possibility of some form of gratification, but I don't think so. From what we know right now, I suspect she saw it as a game of some sort."

"A game?"

"Yes. To see how many victims she could collect, perhaps as a way to prove she was smarter than the police. For what it's worth, and without going into too many details, which you do not want to know, none of her photos show her victims abused. The opposite, in fact.

"The thing I want you to understand is that when it came to her victims, she didn't think or feel about them in the same way we do. We look at the pictures and we feel sick. We don't know what she felt when she looked at them yet. You telling us what you know will help us understand why she did what she did and that might help us stop somebody like her in the future."

"Okay." My voice is shaky. "What do you want to know?"

"What did she tell you her name was?"

"Mazie Maddington."

I see Marcy write the name down.

Al shakes his head. "Interesting, but not even close. Her legal name was Diane Kornis."

"Diane?"

"Kornis. We're guessing that most of the things she told you were lies. We can give you the rundown if you want to keep score."

"Okay."

Marcy looks at me and then starts reading from her notes. "Name: Diane Kornis. Age: thirty. Born: Upstate New York. Only child of only children, so no close relatives."

"She said she had a brother."

Marcy gives me an odd look before continuing. "She came from a well-to-do family. Father was the chief financial officer of a large insurance company. Mother ran a fairly successful organic food store specializing in gluten- and allergy-free products."

"Yuck," says Al.

Marcy ignores him. "Private schools. Well above

average student. Middle school cross-country and swim teams. High school cross-country and golf."

"She was a really good golfer," I volunteer.

Marcy holds up a finger and nods. "Attended a private university on a golf scholarship for the first three years. Well above average student. Major: Psychology with a minor in Languages. State university for graduate school. Well above average student. Major: Behavioral Psychology with master-level courses in Comparative European Literature. Teaching assistant. Masters thesis, um." She puts her finger to the page. "'On the use of micro-expressions, postures, and body language in negotiative situations.' Hired directly from graduate school by the business law firm where she worked until the time of her death. Annual salary with bonuses: low-to-mid-six-figures." She looks at me. "How's the match?"

"Some of it is sort of close. How can you find all this stuff out in just one day?"

"Less than a day," says Al. "They called us after the field office found the list. Hey"—he spreads his arms—"we're the Feds."

"She said her parents were divorced."

Marcy shakes her head and glances at the sheet. "No. He died three years ago from a fall taken while cleaning leaves from the gutters on their summer residence. She died a year later from eating what she thought were edible mushrooms collected on a solo medium-distance hike. Both deaths were ruled accidental."

"She told me about staying out in the country with her divorced dad during the summer."

Another written note. "Her paternal grandparents owned several acres of land with a barn. Horses, that kind of thing."

"Then I guess a lot what she told me was lies."

"That's no surprise. But we'll need those details. Might help our investigation."

Al speaks up. "Kaz, what can you tell us about this brother that we know she didn't have?"

"She didn't tell me his name, or a whole lot about him. I don't know if he was older or not. I know they never got along with each other. He died when she was in college. She didn't seem to miss him very much—at least that's what I thought."

Al lifts his eyebrows and looks at Marcy.

She hesitates, then continues softly. "There's something you need to know. We'd appreciate you staying quiet about it until it's released. We're telling you so you won't be blind-sided, but it's going to be a shock. Okay?"

I nod. Then remember I'm being recorded. "Yeah. Okay."

"Diane was assigned male at birth."

I fuzz out for a few moments. "Male?" I say, quietly.

"Yes. We don't have the test back, yet, but we expect it to show genetic male. The coroner says she had reassignment surgery. She was born..."

I hold up my hand and interrupt. "No! No. Don't tell me. Please. I don't want to know. It's not important. At all."

"I understand. But it'll be in the news, eventually." She turns a page to continue. Then, seeing the look on my face, she reaches over and touches my hand. "Hey. I'm sorry... You doing all right?"

"I don't know how I'm doing."

Marcy frowns. "Listen, Kaz. Don't make a big deal out of any of this gender stuff. It's an interesting data point and nothing more. Remember, it's people who do these things, not genders."

Al shakes his head. "Say that all you want. The crazies will still have a field day."

"Crazies?"

"You have no idea."

"Mazie being trans..." Marcy says. "To us, it's part of who she was, something we'll investigate, to help us understand her better."

"Trouble is," Al frowns, "it makes her an easy target for so-called news outlets, less-than-stellar public figures, and a variety of wilfully obnoxious and loud-mouthed influencers of social media. You'll be a target too, as will your family."

"My family?"

Marcy nods. "Just for being with her. They won't care you were a victim. They'll write, post, and broadcast horrible things about you. All of you. It'll be one of the toughest things you'll ever experience. All of you will probably lose all of your friends and I anticipate a fair number of death threats against you and your family. Some from members of this community. We'll post someone for the first couple of weeks."

"Post...?"

"To keep watch. In case somebody decides to make good on their promise."

I feel my eyes widen. "That happens?"

"Sure does," Al sighs. "We deal with them all the time. Wing nuts spouting lies and claiming it's the truth. Anonymous web cowards daring each other to take some sort of action. Dirt-bags looking to win votes in an election.

"This one'll be bad because it's so high profile. I can hear them now... 'Another example of a sexual deviant grooming and killing innocent children.' What a load of crap. The stats prove that straight, white guys like me are far more dangerous to kids." He tilts his head. "But the crazies, and those who listen to them, don't care about that."

"We'll do our best keep it tamped down," Marcy says, "but I'll tell you now, it won't do much good. The story will be twisted and then fed back on itself until it has nothing to do with reality." She scowls. "Anything to boost the number of views."

"The only good thing about crazies is their short attention spans." Al rubs his face. "We'll also be called liars."

"About what?"

"Mazie. There'll be people on the other side of the fence who refuse to believe she was a killer no matter what evidence we present. Those folks can be noisy, and sometimes they protest, but at least they don't make death threats. Usually."

Marcy smiles a little. "We'll be available to you every step of the way. Do you understand?"

"Yes. I guess."

"May I continue?

I shrug.

"Is that a yes, or a no?"

"A yes. I guess."

"You tell me if it gets too much for you."

"I think I'm mostly numb."

"I can stop."

"No." I shake my head. "Let's get this over with."

She nods at me and goes back to her papers. "Now, from

interviews, we know she began asking classmates to call her Diane near the end of her junior year of college. Her transition caused her to be dropped from the men's golf team. It's why she lost her scholarship.

"There's evidence of voice and movement classes—perhaps to ease her transition or make it more complete—plus some fairly involved hair removal. Her father's insurance records show her surgery took place at the best such clinic in the US during the summer between her college graduation and the start of graduate school. Not an unusual number of post-op visits. Genital, as mentioned. No top surgery—hormones only—I guess, but tracheal shave and"—her eyebrows go up—"rib removal. Which it looks like Dad's insurance paid for." Marcy glances at me. "Did you notice any scars on her neck, under her chin, or on her back?"

She told me the scar on her neck was from falling out of tree when she was a kid. I saw her in a bathing suit. There were no scars on her back. At all."

"She had a good surgeon."

"But, I want to know why me? Why did she pick me?"

"There are..." Marcy pauses "...a wide variety of other photos. All of her victims are much younger than you. All were just entering puberty. But they all have your general body type, besides your height, that is."

"So, they were all thin and, uh, not developed."

She nods. "Mix of female and male. Different races, ethnicities. All apparently choked to death, from the photographic evidence."

I put a hand to my neck. "She used a rear naked choke on me."

Marcy makes a note. "We'll need more detail on that, but it's good to know. It's efficient. Hard to defend against. If applied correctly, the victim is unconscious in seconds and dead shortly thereafter."

"No kidding."

"Um, sorry. The other thing you and the younger victims seem to have in common is pierced ears. Newly pierced for the boy in the pond—the holes weren't healed. The photos show them all wearing the same earrings given to you.

"In fact, downstate, about three years ago, a man who got lost searching for a geocache stumbled across the scattered, skeletonized remains of who we think was this female." She taps another one of the images. "An earring was found at the scene. Back then, we did a facial reconstruction, but had no luck with her DNA so she's remained unidentified. With actual photos, we might get some hits. We're not sure of the symbolism involved with the diamond and ruby. May be as obvious as her marking her victims as part of her collection. But it may be obscure. Maybe she just liked the style."

A chill runs down my spine. "Wait. Boy in the pond? Mazie told me it was a female friend."

"Not true. Were there any other gifts?"

"The earrings, prepaid phone, T-shirt, and a pair of jeans."

"May we examine them?"

"You can have them!"

"Thanks."

Al speaks up. "We don't think she intended you as one of her victims. You don't fit her pattern, unless you are a whole other pattern which we think is highly unlikely." A very small shrug. "Anyway...the boy from the pond has already been identified. His family, three hours away by car, by the way, didn't have a clue as to what happened to him and insist he wasn't the type to keep secrets. We didn't find any social media evidence of interactions between the two leading up to the pond killing."

"She used a messaging app that she said left no trace."

Marcy makes a note. "We'll need more information on that."

Al continues. "So, at the moment, and depending on what we find in this app, we don't think there was any sort of long-term relationships or grooming with her victims. Meet—Gift—Death. Maybe in that order, maybe not, but all over a short period of time. Hours, perhaps. Probably picked out a child and stalked them. For some, the chase is as important as anything else. She was smart and careful, that's for sure. There's no telling how long she might've continued except for you finding that earring. Years. Decades, maybe."

"So, if she wasn't going to kill me, what was I?

The woman shifts in her seat. "You are unique in that matter. There was her work, and her *savate,* at which she excelled..."

"What's *savate*?"

"French kickboxing. Real kickboxing, not the fake exercise stuff. She held a silver glove three. That's a mid-level competition rank. All of her coworkers and gym-mates spoke highly of her. They couldn't tell us much, except that she was smart, private, and extremely particular. 'Control freak' was the phrase most often used to describe her along with variations of 'OCD' and 'ice queen.' The last especially among the men. Competitive. A very sore loser. But, as far as we can tell, she had no social life."

"Mazie told me she had lots of, uh, experience."

"Sexually?" Marcy shakes her head. "Don't think so. We found a few flirtations but no serious lovers, ex- or otherwise. A couple of one-nighters and some short-terms with different people before, during, and after transition, some facilitated by various internet apps. One of those people had Maddington as a surname—we'll look a little closer at them.

But that's about it. In fact, she had no real friends."

"Sort of like me."

The two exchange glances. Al leans in. "And what do we need to know about you?"

"Don't you already know?"

He smiles. Crooked teeth. "Give us a break, Kaz, we've been on the case for less than a day."

"I'm gender dysphoric, on pubertal blockers, and I isolate."

"That makes you the 'unnamed teenager' in the news articles we saw. Did she know that?"

"Yes. I told her."

Again, Marcy and Al look at each other.

"That's the hook." Al sits back. "Don't you think, Marce?"

Looking at me like Mazie did the people on the beach, she nods. "Yeah. A transitional state between herself and her victims. A near-equal adult in a child-like body."

"Hey—I'm sitting right here—I can hear you, y'know!"

"Did she use it to manipulate you?"

"Now that I know, yes. I didn't see it when it was happening."

Al sort of laughs. "She made a way better living than we ever will by making smart, rich guys do what they didn't want to do. Those skills? Those looks? Getting her undivided attention? Nobody would stand a chance." He grins. "Not even me."

"Especially not you." Marcy smiles. Then, to me. "Did she take you places? Locations she seemed to think of as special?"

"How'd you know that?"

"We'll need to know those locations. That's where we'll start looking for other victims. Some killers are very proud of what they do. They know they can't display their accomplishments but still want to show off. Sometimes they enjoy the fact that people are close to their handiwork, but still can't see it. Like you and the boy in the pond." She moves her hands back and forth. "It's a control thing. Many of them get a kick out of it: simultaneously taking and keeping power over the viewer and the victim."

She sighs and runs her fingertips through her short hair. "We have pictures of twenty-three, and there are twenty-three on the list. One identified and another likely found. It's a start. The photos show a number of different backgrounds. She traveled for her work and on vacations. No telling where the others are or how long they've been there. We'll put the images up and run them. Hope for the best. Until we break her code, it'll be tough."

"Did she ever talk about places she wanted to go?" Al asks.

"No. Where we went was always a surprise. She never told me where she was, except sometimes for work. I didn't know where she lived, and I never even asked."

"It was more than an hour from here, near the airport. And had you asked, she would've lied. Secrecy was part of her control." Al continues. "Did she push your limits?"

I nod. "Yeah, big time. But I thought she was doing it to teach me things."

"May I ask what?"

I squirm in my seat and know I'm reddening. "Some sex stuff. But also, things about golf. And people. How not to be nervous and awkward. She was always telling me to be brave and stand up straight. That I could do more than I thought I could. And that I was better than I thought I was. I liked that about her."

"Pygmalion?" Al asks Marcy.

"For sure." Marcy replies. "Turned to Frankenstein, though."

"What?"

"Never mind," he says. "Sometimes good to you, then?"

"Yeah. She was a good teacher."

Marcy rattles the papers she's holding. "She was an assistant in grad school, remember? An excellent one, according to her professors."

"I thought Mazie and I were having a good time."

"You were," Al says. "But not for the same reasons."

"You need to know anything else? I really need to sit and start figuring all this out."

"We're almost done. Did you know she had a second vehicle?"

"No," I say, surprised. "I only ever saw her drive Fancy Car, uh, a fancy car. It was almost new, electric, fast."

"The one she was driving when your friend was killed?"

"Yeah."

"They're pulling the GPS data from it as we speak. It might give us some useful information. She also had an older domestic sedan. Not new, not electric, not fast. And no GPS. A very clean set of digging tools in the trunk."

"Was it red?"

"Yes. How'd you know?"

"Just a guess."

Al grins. "Want my job?"

"Finally," Marcy says. "We want to ask you about the moments leading up to her death."

"I already told the police about that."

"We have specific questions."

"Like?"

"Did you have any idea there was a body in the pond?"

"No. None."

"Why did you lead her there?"

"I was trying to get her to face the truth about the person whose ashes she told me were spread there. To admit that she loved them. So she'd feel better."

"Did you have any idea the earring was there?"

"No."

"How do you think it got there?"

"I..."

Marcy raises her eyebrows at me.

"Y'know, I didn't plan to go down to the pond. I figured Mazie wouldn't do it because she hated being near dirty water, bugs, and stuff like that. But I stumbled at the top of the hill and sort of pulled her along with me. And the earring... If I had been a little bit one way or the other... My fingers just sort of...found it. How it got there, I have no idea." I hear myself speaking quieter. "I know the body was under all that water. The earring was there and I found it. Luck, I guess. Plain old luck."

"Lucky for her future victims, that's for sure."

"May I ask a question?"

"Sure. Shoot."

"When I found the earring, why did she lose it and attack me? I mean, why didn't she get in her car and try to escape?"

Marcy speaks up. "She was all about control and confrontation. She lived what she probably thought was a perfect life in a perfect world under her perfect control. You finding that earring took that away from her, all at once. She reacted the same way a small mean child would if you knocked over her wonderfully constructed house of blocks. Once she suffered any loss of control, it was like a dam breaking. She couldn't control that either, which only made her worse."

Al chimes in. "Don't forget she hated to lose. And she probably thought she was smarter than everybody else, right?"

"Yeah, she was always saying the world was full of idiots."

He nods. "Right. But now you, not a person, mind you, but a plaything she has been manipulating, shows intelligence equal or superior to her own. You're suddenly smart and she finds herself as the idiot. Maybe she couldn't process the experience."

Marcy continues. "You dislocating her wrist—nice move, by the way—you dislocating her wrist was more than she could take. You topped her mentally, then seriously challenged her physically. You're lucky to be alive, Kaz. If she had managed to get her hands on you, as sure as we're sitting here, you'd be dead."

"Dead. What do you think would've happened if I never found the earring?"

Marcy gives me a sad smile and speaks gently. "I'm going to guess that she was special to you, right? And that you thought she felt the same way about you?"

"Yeah."

"It's easy to see why that would be, and I know it's hard to accept, but she was never who or what you thought she was. She lied to you. She manipulated you to lead you to those feelings. It doesn't mean you're stupid. It means she was very, very good at a game most people never play. I know that doesn't make you feel any better, but it's the truth and you need to keep that in mind. Can you try to do that?"

"I guess I can."

"So, with all of that going on, I bet she would've strung you along, broken your heart, sat back, and enjoyed watching you suffer."

"And I would've thought *that* was bad."

"It would've been bad because she would've returned to adding to her list. I know you don't feel like one, Kaz. But you are a hero."

"You're right, I don't feel like one. But thanks."

Marcy softens. "Giving a family closure, even a tragic one, is a blessing. That's also thanks to you. You remember that too."

My heart lifts, a little, in a broken sort of way. "I'll try." I sigh.

"Almost done. When she attacked you, she had a seizure?"

"I never used that word. I don't know what to call it. She didn't move or sound like she normally did. It was almost like she was a puppet, only out of control or broken." I blink at the memory.

"This word—" She looks at her notes. "'Kazabee.' What does it mean to you?"

"It's a nickname a good friend had for me."

"The friend who was accidentally struck and killed by Diane?"

I look at the floor. "Yes. Jimmy."

"And you are sure that's what she said?"

"Yes."

"And you are sure you never mentioned that name to her?"

I look Marcy in the eyes. "Dead sure."

She stares back. "How do you think she knew it?"

"I don't know." I shrug. "Maybe Jimmy's ghost told her."

Al takes over. "This flash you say you saw."

My defenses rise. "I didn't say I saw it. I *saw* it."

He holds up a hand. "Relax, Kaz. We know the officers you spoke to were...reluctant to believe your account. Honestly, can you blame them?"

"No. I guess not."

"So, this flash. Was there a sound with it?"

"Not that I remember."

Marcy refers to her notes. "You told the officer that 'she looked like she bounced off a wall.' Is that true?"

"Yes."

Al scratches under his right ear with his left hand. "You know her cause of death?"

"A skull fracture, right? That's what I saw. From where her head hit the dam." I look from one to the other. "Right?"

His expression never changes. "Officially, yes, that'll be the cause. We can't figure what happened with this flash, but something sure as hell did. Her head never hit the dam. The coroner said the fracture was from the inside out and that her eyes and brains looked like they had been boiled."

I manage to open the car door in time.

Al waits until I'm done retching. "This'll be a Grade-A shit show when it hits the fan. I advise you to stay away from social media. And you tell us about the death threats. You understand?"

"Yeah," I say, wiping my mouth with the tissue Marcy hands me. "No social media and you get the death threats. I understand."

Chapter Fifteen

SK'DOO

"I loved him more than my own life."

"I never wanted to fight in that war."

"I was bought and sold. Like an animal."

I find myself near Lyman, the same as when Edge lightninged me for flying in the bird.

I seem the same but don't know how I could be. I was. Then I wasn't. Now I am. How could I be who I think I am? Is this Dead?

I remember pushing myself into Mazie's head, then... nothing. I zoom to Pond to see if Kazabee is safe.

Once I get there, I know I'm not me because these are things I didn't see. I can't go past Ezme because old Edge is back. There's yellow and red banners everywhere. I can see that Pat is no longer in Pond because Pond is almost empty of water. The Quicks must have taken it out to find all of Pat. Maybe they were looking for more Deads. But I know there are no more.

When did this happen? How did I not see? I either wasn't here, or I saw it and don't remember, but that never happens, does it? I remember everything.

The grass around Pond is torn and dirty. Sitting with a dark, trampled, muddy bottom, Pond looks...sad. I know the water will be back. But I'll know it'll not be the same. It'll look like Pond, but it won't be. Like I'm like me, but I'm not.

I don't do things that hurt, but all of this is because of me. I hurt Kazabee, Pond, the turtles, Mazie, me, Edge. I did all of this!

"Everyone takes their own blame. That's what Gramma says."

Ezme always says the right thing. I suddenly know none of what I see is because of me. Mazie put Pat in Pond, where he didn't belong. Everything else was because of that.

I hope Kazabee is safe. I hope the turtles are safe.

Chapter Sixteen

KAZ

Marcy and Al interview me several times over the next few days. It's Marcy I talk to, along with anybody else in the family who wants to sit and listen. Friends don't keep secrets. I don't give all the gory details about the sex but answer her questions. The one thing I refuse to do is go with them to Eastdale. They take pictures and videos of the area surrounding the now-empty pond and we talk about them instead. There's red and yellow police warning tape all over the place.

When GeeGeema discovers Al grew up less than twenty

miles from where she was born, he becomes her prisoner. The two of them, together, are like a family reunion. Whooping it up, trading stories, and watching old movies.

He promises he'll look after me and keep me safe a thousand times. She sure is disappointed when they leave. When she asks if he's handsome, I lie and tell her that he isn't toady-looking.

*

Al was right: It *was* a Grade-A shit show.

I quit my job. Mr. Amolsch tried to get me to stay, but I couldn't. Even then, nobody at the store talked about me. Mr. Amolsch wouldn't say anything. Ms. Collins scolded a TV reporter like they were a naughty second-grader. Sarah told another to shove his microphone up his ass. They bleeped the word, but you could still see what she said. That made me laugh. But after the first couple of days, I turned off the news and never went back.

I tried looking up Diane Kornis and found hardly anything from before the body in the pond. One small article and a tiny low-res five-year-old picture of her in New York, taken after some C-Suite deal. At least what she told me about her job and paying to scrub the Internet was true.

But, after they pulled the body from the pond, all her names were all over. Mine too.

Everyone in the family had to change their phone numbers and email addresses. I changed mine twice.

The death threats started after the stories about Mazie's gender transition hit the web. We passed each of them on to Marcy and Al. We all stopped using any social media and went to flip-phones. We only answered when we knew the number and let the others roll to deactivated voicemails. The people Marcy and Al had sit in the black sedan at the end of the block left after two-and-a-half weeks. I was sort of glad to see them go.

What people posted about both Mazie and me was so...disturbing. Idiots will say anything when they're not saying it to your face. I hope they all rot in hell.

When I mentioned it to Al, he said he knew somebody who knew somebody. Over the next three weeks, search results on my name dropped from the hundreds of thousands to almost nothing. That was pretty sweet—and kind of scary.

I had all kinds of offers for interviews: online, cable, podcasts, news, talk shows. All that stuff. Turned them all down. People asked if they could write my life story and sell it as a script for a movie. That was a big hell no!

I kept getting followed by reporters. A lawyer stopped that, but it didn't help much. Instead of me, they interviewed people who said they knew me. What they said about me was all over everything, over and over and over again. But, like the other posts, they just sort of disappeared.

I refused to leave the house. Everyone avoided us and my parents lost most of their friends. We all ended up in counseling, except GeeGeema who said it was nowhere near as bad as being threatened with a rope and a tree.

I was creeped out but mostly happy when they started finding the victims: buried in the field past the old gas station, hidden in a culvert near the driving range, parts of a skeleton in the stream down from the old mill. Said that way, it sounds like they were easy to locate. Nothing could be further from the truth. In the end, they found nobody at the beach.

Each victim, we got a call from Marcy or Al before the news was released. So we'd be ready for the blast of publicity.

Al was excited when he called to tell me they finally broke Mazie's code. He said "somebody even dumber than him" realized that the list also described some paperweights they found at her home. By grouping them together and comparing them to the text, it helped decode things like colors, shapes, and numbers used for size measurements.

All the weights were handmade. Many were one of a kind. By finding where they were made and sold, they learned some of the locations. After that, it got easier.

The first victim they found using the list was buried

beside an interstate highway near Columbus, Ohio. The others, or at least evidence of them, were all over the country. Mazie surprised us by using Spanish for a location in Los Angeles, but she did use French, for one in Quebec. Two in northern Italy were in German. That caused calls from police and press in those places, and I had to change my email and phone for the third time. After that, things died down. It turned out Al was right... Crazies have short attention spans.

The dates showed she started during her last year of graduate school, giving Marcy and Al someplace to begin.

Mazie's list also contained the full names of the children. All of those families had to give up hope. But at least they knew. I had to remind myself it was a good thing.

Probably most heart-breaking were the letters and packages from the families of some of the kids. A few were angry, but most held stories of happy times. All of them contained pictures. Many started with "I don't know why I'm writing you." The lawyer responded to them. I was told not to, but I read every one and put them in a box to keep forever.

How had I fallen in love with somebody who did such terrible things? Learned so much from someone as twisted as she was? The worst part was that all those kids were dead but I was still alive.

I couldn't believe I was too dumb to see what Mazie was doing, that I had been fooled so badly. I had enjoyed being held and touched by the hands that killed so many kids. I kept washing my skin raw but never felt clean.

I wasn't sure I was going to make it, even with all the counseling. I hacked my hair so short and so badly that it made Mom cry. I took the mirror in my room off the wall and hid it in my closet. It was so hard to keep from cutting. I don't know how, but I managed not to give myself any new scars, even with resting a blade against my skin so many times. It took two months before I could sleep without a light. Even longer for the dreams to stop.

Gradually, I started to accept that I had nothing to do with it. Mazie made her choices, and I was swept along. *She* was the murderer. She didn't kill me like she killed the others because, for whatever reasons, that's what she decided.

I didn't have anything to do with any of those things. It was her. All of it. Her. I was a victim, except I was alive. Like Al said, nobody stood a chance against her. And like Marcy said, it was me who managed to stop the killings.

Through it all GeeGeema made sure that I got up, got dressed, made my bed every day, took a shower every so often, and that each and every one of my snot-rags ended up in the trash can. She and I watched so much TV together. We never really talked about what happened but spending time with her and taking care of Preston helped as much as anything else.

By the time my hair had grown enough for my cowlick to show, my mirror was back where it was supposed to be. I could even watch golf.

I home-schooled for a semester which I kind of liked. When I asked for a calculus tutor, Angel volunteered. She was a great teacher and I managed better-than-passing grades. For me, it was like some sort of miracle.

She told me that she liked working Carts and Parking Lot because it helped keep her in shape and it didn't matter at all if she was short and methodical—her word for slow. And she knew Sarah was dropping change but didn't say anything since she liked the extra money. I promised not to tell.

She turned into a good friend: smart, patient, and funny. She and GeeGeema adored each other, they celebrated their birthdays together—eighty years and one day apart. Preston even sat in her lap! For like two minutes. No pictures, but it still happened.

She seemed happy to turn her phone off when we were together, like I asked. And once I was brave enough to start, it was easy to talk to her about the stuff that happened to me. She couldn't believe she had walked by me on the beach until I described her bathing suit. We actually laughed about that! She said she used SPF-100.

We started riding bikes together. One day Mr. Mazza waved us down and gave us each a yellow rose, complete with thorns.

Angel and I left the flowers with Jimmy. His new grave-stone was there. Then, with the squirrels following us, she helped me visit the pond for the first time since Mazie died. I showed her where I found the earring and described what happened. She hugged me when I began to shake and cry. I had a rough night after that. Then things started getting better.

*

SK'DOO

I'm...happy when I finally see Kazabee. She's with a Quick I've never seen but who I think is her friend. They put flowers on Dead Jimmy's grave then sit close on the bench near Ottmar, hold hands, and talk.

They have no lightning-boxes and I want to get close, but I don't because I'm...afraid. I don't understand, but it's true.

I follow as they go to Pond. I watch from Ezme. I want to be a little closer, but Edge stops me. I want to listen, to find out what happened, but they talk so quietly. I see

Kazabee point to where she found the earring. I know she's telling her story.

Even so far apart, I feel Kazabee's confusion, anger, fright, bravery, and sadness all rolled into one. And when she starts to cry, like I knew she would, her friend hugs her. They climb Hill, sit on the bench across the road, still out of reach, and tell each other it will be all right.

I hope so. For all of us. And Pond. And the turtles.

When the two Quicks leave, the Deads and me watch them go. I hope, with enough visits, I'll learn to not be afraid.

Chapter Seventeen

KAZ

I finally asked Angel the same questions about being female that I had asked Mazie. It was nice to be able to trust her answers.

One afternoon, she gave me my first *true* kiss. At the kitchen table, after a calc lesson, when I told her I liked her freckles and thought her green eyes were pretty.

It was on my right cheek. When I blushed, she giggled. That made me blush more.

It was a little past two o'clock in the afternoon on November 24th, and it was cold and rainy, and I'll remember it forever.

Not too long after that I called Mr. Amolsch and asked if I could start back to work. It was scary at first, but they were glad to see me, and I was happy to be there. Jimmy's replacement was one of Sarah's younger cousins from the next town over. They're okay.

I also decided to go off my meds. I only told those who are important to me because my business is my business. I'm still scared of what's going to happen to me, but I have my family and friends to help. Besides, if I've learned anything over the past few months, it's that I can always change what I don't like.

Chapter Eighteen

KAZ

I touch the silver polliwog before leaving my room. Mazie... Diane might've been crazy, but she was smart.

"Morning, GeeGeema."

"Good morning, glory. It's good to have you up and about."

"Where's Preston?"

"Don't know. But he'll show when you open the can."

"You like some water?

"Yes, please, and thank you. Now, let me give you a hug and a look-see."

"GeeGeema, you know you can't see."

"Whoever told you that was a liar!"

"I suppose so. I gotta get going."

"You be safe now. You dressed warm enough?"

"Yes, I'm dressed fine. And I'll be safe. I promise. Bye-bye."

"And I love you too!"

Going back to finish school is hard. But I am brave and I will stand up straight and I won't let the idiots take anything from me. They know I'm learning to box. That'll help.

I think, maybe on my way home, I'll ride Eastdale's outside road. I can do that on my own now. Just like I can go through the parking lot at work. I'll never forget what happened in either of those places, but I can deal with it.

*

SK'DOO

A new burial with no stone moved Edge not too long ago. In Damps, by Outside Road, as far away from Olive Mae Wilson as it can be. I can now reach a small corner of the woods near new Pond. And I can see the other side of Silas again. That's good.

It's quiet, here, so far away from the other graves. I've been sitting with this new Dead but they're not a talker. Not much has been said. Not even a name.

"*I like to collect.*"

About Don Hilton

Don Hilton was raised the second of three sons in a small Pennsylvania town. Easily bored, his life has been a broad mix of experiences. He's struggled with the blues and is pleased that time grants some measure of peace. He prefers his peanut butter sandwiches with strawberry jam.

Email

dhilton-writer@outlook.com

Facebook

www.facebook.com/dhiltonbooks

Instagram

www.instagram.com/donhiltonbooks/

Website

www.dhiltonbooks.net

Connect with NineStar Press

www.ninestarpress.com

www.facebook.com/ninestarpress

www.twitter.com/ninestarpress

www.instagram.com/ninestarpress

Made in the USA
Columbia, SC
01 July 2024

37948378R00180